Return to Q'ehazi

THE Q'EHAZI TRILOGY: BOOK 2

MADISON C. BRIGHTWELL

Copyright © 2025 Madison C. Brightwell.

All rights reserved. No part of this book may be reproduced, stored, or transmitted by any means—whether auditory, graphic, mechanical, or electronic—without written permission of both publisher and author, except in the case of brief excerpts used in critical articles and reviews. Unauthorized reproduction of any part of this work is illegal and is punishable by law.

ISBN: 979-8-89419-742-5 (sc)
ISBN: 979-8-89419-743-2 (hc)
ISBN: 979-8-89419-744-9 (e)

Because of the dynamic nature of the Internet, any web addresses or links contained in this book may have changed since publication and may no longer be valid. The views expressed in this work are solely those of the author and do not necessarily reflect the views of the publisher, and the publisher hereby disclaims any responsibility for them.

One Galleria Blvd., Suite 1900, Metairie, LA 70001
(504) 702-6708

For my husband, Ray, my constant support.

ENDORSEMENTS AND REVIEWS for "The World Beyond the Redbud Tree", the first in the trilogy.

Madison Brightwell has created a tantalizing, mystical tale filled with suspense and adventure. She skillfully portrays the characters' mindsets and feelings with great depth and has the unique gift of bringing her reader into the world she creates in such a way that the reader will feel as if they are actually part of the story itself and invested in the outcome.

—CC Tillery, author of "Beloved Woman" Series of Books

BY AMAZON READERS

This book is a gem. It's a captivating journey into a parallel world that's as enchanting and thought-provoking. The main character, Charli, navigates a world of pain and hope, and her journey to a peaceful, otherworldly society offers a refreshing escape. It's a beautifully written and an uplifting read.

This book is more than just a fantasy; it's a powerful story of healing and self-discovery. Charli's journey will resonate with anyone who has faced challenges and sought a better understanding of themselves and the world around them. If you're looking for a thought-provoking read that blends alternate history with personal growth, "The World Beyond the Redbud Tree" is definitely worth your time.

Madison C. Brightwell's novel is a masterpiece of imaginative storytelling, weaving together the trials of Charli's reality with the utopian dreams of Q'ehazi. Brightwell's narrative is not just a tale of escape, but a beacon of inspiration, urging readers to reflect on creating a better world. Engaging, heartfelt, and beautifully written, this book is a must-read for anyone seeking a glimpse of grace amidst life's challenges.

Chapter One

Charli's eyes were stinging and raw from weeping. When she inhaled, her breath came in heaving gasps, and when she exhaled, she released sighing sobs to express her emotions. Nobody was there to witness her pain. She felt a cool breeze caress her face as if it had been sent to comfort her, and she closed her eyes momentarily to let this reassurance permeate her being.

Her fights with Nick were getting more and more frequent, and this one was the worst. Charli replayed it in her mind, as if she was watching a movie scene playing on repeat, and she believed she could better understand it by watching it over and over again.

The back-and-forth dialogue she was having with herself was mostly internal, although occasionally some unbidden words fell from her lips. She had no need to be embarrassed, though, as only the trees and the grass heard her.

"I understand why he was angry, but he doesn't have to yell at me like that. He has no right to be angry, anyway. It's not my fault I'm not pregnant. I didn't ask for a negative reading. I didn't do it on purpose! Damn him!"

"Yes, but it wasn't that you weren't *pregnant* that bothered him. It was that you were *relieved* you weren't going to have *his* kid."

"But he always said he *never wanted* a kid. He should make up his mind."

"He doesn't want a kid. His male ego was hurt, and he felt insulted."

"Ugh, what an asshole!"

"Most men would feel the same way. Let's face it, you don't love him enough to want to have his child, even if he had agreed to help you take care of it."

"Maybe I don't. But it's not about that. It's about the fact that he absolutely refuses to take responsibility for anything. Can you imagine him as a father? He'd be the worst. I had always vowed I'd never raise a kid on my own. I know it wasn't my mom's fault that my dad died when I was 12, but that really messed me up. I never want to do that to my own kid. So, yes I was relieved that I didn't have to make that decision. I want a kid, sure, but for the right reasons and at the right time. I should *not* go against my own principles just to make that asshole happy."

"If he's such an asshole, why are you still going out with him?"

Charli sniffed back her tears and grinned at the absurdity of this question. *Why, indeed?*

She took the pregnancy test out of her pocket and looked again at the faint pink line—a negative result—and she remembered her crushing first reaction: disappointment. She was secretly hoping she would become a mother, and she would love to have a child to guide and teach everything she knew about life. Just not right now and certainly not with *him*.

Charli threw the test to the ground in disgust. Why on earth had she chosen to be with this man, who she knew from the beginning was incapable of fulfilling her needs for security and commitment? She wasn't an idiot. She had noticed right away his selfish and unreliable character. Yet she'd been seduced by his charming persona and handsome face. Even worse, she believed in his lies against her better judgment.

Charli breathed deeply and closed her eyes once more. When she let go of the negative thoughts that tormented her and just focused on the peaceful sounds and smells surrounding her, here in this nature park in the middle of the city where she was completely alone, she felt blanketed by serenity. After all, nothing bad was happening to her right now in this moment.

Charli leaned back again and became lost in her thoughts that were more meandering now and less like jagged daggers out to hurt her with their piercing accusations. She wondered if it was time now to leave Nick. She would be going home soon anyway, which would make the break-up easier. The idea of not seeing him anymore or having to put up with his diatribes against her and constant demeaning remarks created more relief than regrets.

She'd come here to relax and get away and feel nature's consolation, and it was starting to take effect. As she surveyed the grass and the trees and the sky all around her, she felt that her problems were small, as small as *she* was in the vast scheme of things in the universe and that was reassuring and comforting.

The wound in the man's leg was oozing so much blood it was difficult to find the cut. Joslyn tried to staunch the flow with a tourniquet, and the man winced in pain, but he refused to cry out. He simply grimaced and took short, labored breaths.

"Hurry up, dammit" he snarled. He was an older man with the grizzled appearance of somebody who had been a warrior in his youth, and the attitude of somebody familiar with being in command. His iron-gray hair stood out in clumps from his head, as if surprised to still be adorning that large bearish face with its permanently disgruntled expression.

Joslyn remarked, "I have to stop the bleeding."

The old man replied, "What you have to do is get the lump out, the hard metal pellet. Can't you see it?"

"Pellet? But how on earth did this happen?"

"Just get it out. Get it out!"

The wound was so deep, deeper than anything Joslyn had ever seen, and he'd treated many wounds before, usually accidental knife cuts and the like, but never anything like this.

"It's going to hurt," Joslyn warned. He was aware that the man was significantly older than he was—possibly in his sixties according to the lines on his face—and Joslyn didn't want to cause him any more suffering than was necessary.

"I know, I know, I can take it," the man stated, gritting his teeth in anticipation of the agony to come.

"I can give you something."

"No, just do it and do it fast!"

Complying with the man's request, Joslyn dug into the wound using his surgical knife with speed and precision, and he eventually extracted the hard metal object.

Once this procedure was completed, the older man sighed and laid on the bed to let Joslyn clean and dress the wound. His breathing became easier, and his blanched face started to regain its color.

Joslyn offered the man a cup of hot tea made with the *Pukatl* herb to aid in the healing, but the man refused the drink, saying "I don't believe in that stuff."

Once he had revived sufficiently, Joslyn's patient asked to see the metal object taken out of his thigh, and Joslyn obliged.

"That's incredible!" the man exclaimed, surveying its metal surface with wonder.

"What is that, and how did it get in your leg?" asked Joslyn.

"I'm not here to tell you my life story, you know," the older man snapped. "It's your job to put me back together."

Joslyn surveyed the invalid calmly, wondering why he seemed so on edge. Since most of Joslyn's patients were known to him, it was unusual to be treating a stranger, but he never turned anyone away who needed help. This man was dressed in clothes that were unlike anything Joslyn had seen before. He appeared to be wearing some sort of uniform, as his jacket and pants were matching and made of heavy cloth that must have been uncomfortably warm in the summer months. Joslyn was used to observing people closely, both because of his profession and his natural inclination to look beneath the surface when dealing with those in need of help, whether emotional or physical. He noticed that this man had a slight twitch in his left eye that betrayed a certain nervousness he undoubtedly tried to hide.

Joslyn responded to the man's irritable comment with a polite statement rather than any retort.

"That's true, and I have endeavored to do that. I was just curious, as I've never seen anything like that before."

"It was an accident."

"I see," replied Joslyn, not expecting more explanation; however, the man seemed to wish to unburden himself, and Joslyn was accustomed to listening.

"It's called a gun," the older man said with an odd pride in his voice.

"What is this gun?"

"This thing that injured me. It's a weapon, and it shoots out these metal pellets, so much faster than your bows and arrows. It can literally kill a man instantly."

Joslyn couldn't contain a look of horror. "Why would anybody want to *kill* a man?"

The older man didn't answer this question and simply repeated, "It was an accident. Barylos was practicing, and she didn't realize what happened."

"Barylos?" exclaimed Joslyn.

"Yes," admitted the man, still wearing that odd prideful look. "I'm one of her Liberation Warriors. I didn't tell you at first because I thought you might not treat me if you knew."

"Of course, I'd have treated you, it's my job, I don't turn anybody away."

"Even one of your expelled sister's followers?" the man offered in sneering tones.

"She's my half-sister."

"Oh, yes?"

"Abbe and I are from the same father, but Barylos' father was someone my mother was with for a short time only when she took a trip abroad."

It wasn't until the visit was over and the man left that Joslyn realized they had conducted their entire business aloud, and they did not use any of the "thought connection" that people usually used when they wanted one-on-one communication. Then he remembered what he had heard about these people, the "Liberation Warriors" as the man had called them. They no longer communicated psychically with their thoughts but only with words spoken aloud. They also rejected the use of the *Pukatl* herb, either for healing or even for daily consumption like the rest of the Q'ehazi took it. They didn't believe in the ways of peace or attaining a *State of Grace*. They renounced all of the Q'ehazi teachings and refused to follow Sovereign Aurora. Since they had all been excommunicated, they lived far away, in a place that Joslyn knew little about, except that it was far to the north at the edge of the continent in lands most Q'ehazi had never seen or visited. The land was as inhospitable as the people who resided there.

Joslyn continued to ponder on his interactions with this man, even as he treated the other patients who came to see him that day. A mother from the Village of the Teachers Northeast brought in the twin babies that Joslyn had helped to deliver a few months before, as they were suffering from colic and she needed some herbs to ease their pain. A colleague of his from the Village of Healers had been dealing with some grief over the loss of his best friend in an accident where he'd been thrown off his horse and Joslyn not only gave his colleague some herbal remedies, but he also gave him the comfort of a listening and sympathetic ear. It was a typical day in the life for Joslyn, but with the added ingredient of a stranger who had come from the world Joslyn knew little about, where his half-sister had ensconced herself, for what purpose he didn't know.

Joslyn was not a person to judge people harshly, as that wasn't in his nature, plus he'd been raised to value empathy and compassion. But the exchange with one of the Barylos people had disturbed him and disrupted his peace of mind, so this was something he knew he could talk over with the other members of his family to whom he was close.

The sweet early summer air was calling him from outside, and Joslyn inhaled deeply as he stepped out of the front door of his clinic. His preference would have been to work outside all the time, but in order to maintain hygiene, he conducted most of his medical practice indoors. Despite the fact that abundant windows let in plenty of light throughout the day, he often felt the need to feel the ground beneath his feet and commune with nature for a few moments during his workday.

Earlier in the year, one of his friends from the Village of the Farmers Southeast had planted some colorful pollinator plants and flowers in garden boxes that created an ever-changing display of beauty and form as entrancing as any art exhibit. Momentarily, he was captivated by the dance of two huge orange butterflies as they capered around each other and then flew to distant parts of the garden to feast on more succulent petals. It was late morning, and Joslyn turned his face to the slowly rising sun as it soared toward its zenith in the sky and cast a gentle warmth on his dark-brown skin.

As his eyes were closed, he became aware of the thought-words before they were accompanied by a voice he knew well, "Joslyn, I need to see you now."

Darting his head to the left in the direction of the sound, and blinking his eyes open again, he became aware of the unexpected visitor who was approaching with a swift and urgent gait.

"Millai, I am glad of your visit. How can I help?" Joslyn gave the standard response to all his visiting patients, with an additional warmth because this was a woman he knew well.

The young woman was short in stature, with pale skin and wild curly red hair that stood out from her elfin face, giving her the impression of being a child. Yet she had a voice that was more mature, and she had a note of urgency in her tone that alerted Joslyn. Upon reaching him, she threw her arms around him and gave him a hug that was brief but intense. "I wasn't sure what to do. Serai suggested I come and see you."

Joslyn widened his eyes in slight surprise, "Well, I'm glad of it. Come inside."

He ushered her into the clinic and showed her to the comfortable armchair where he always sought to relax his patients while listening to their troubles and deciding on a course of treatment. Millai's shoulders relaxed as soon as she took up her position in the chair, and this allowed her story to flow from her in an outpouring of fear and sorrow. The young woman explained that she'd been experiencing some chronic pain in her shoulders and neck for the past two weeks. She wondered if it was something to do with the dreams she kept having, of her boyfriend abandoning her, that had her waking up every morning in a cold sweat. She and he had been arguing recently because he wanted to have children and she didn't. Millai was torn between wanting to please him and desiring to pursue her passion for gardening and discovering new varieties of plants and vegetables that could help people in the future. She bowed her head in relief when Joslyn validated her concerns and told her to follow her passions.

Joslyn explained that the physical symptoms and the emotional dreams were likely linked. He encouraged her to go to the Dreams Academy for some interpretations that might help. Even though the Academy had been leaderless for some time, its extensive library had books and teachings on the subject. Joslyn prescribed some herbs and tinctures made from medicinal plants and useful for topical application on the affected shoulder.

Joslyn couldn't resist asking about Serai's well-being since she had not been mentioned yet. Millai smiled a small inscrutable smile at hearing her sister's name mentioned.

"She is well." Then added, "She still misses you, of course."

Joslyn smiled in response, but said nothing, not quite knowing the correct words. A pang of guilt hit him in the chest at the sudden recognition of the pain he must have caused his ex-girlfriend after he abandoned her. Even though quiet and seemingly compliant, Joslyn was not one to change his mind and he still felt sure he'd made the right decision.

"Thank you so much," gushed Millai upon receiving her medications. "I have tomatoes for you in payment. I know how much you like them, and we've had a bumper crop this year." She reached inside her basket and pulled out a bag full of the luscious ripe fruit.

Joslyn thanked her for the payment. He loved tomatoes and knew couldn't finish all of them himself, so he was happy to have something to share at dinner with his mother and the others that evening.

Joslyn finished his work and walked over to see his mother, father, and sister and to sit and eat dinner with them along with some others from the village. As it was just a mile or so, his long legs carried him swiftly over the grass and through the trees to reach the clearing at the Village of Farmers where a communal dinner was being enjoyed that evening. Since his recent break-up with his now ex-girlfriend of three years, he had spent most of his time outside of work either socializing with friends or enjoying time with members of his close and extended family.

As he approached the long table where people had gathered to dine, Joslyn received a warm welcome from members of the village. After conversing a little with friends and exchanging pleasantries using the customary thought-words, he sat next to his younger sister, Abbe, and his mother, Sovereign Aurora, who sat at the head of the table. Joslyn's father, Serano, sat at the other end of the table and was as usual in his own reverie and not interacting much with the other diners.

Joslyn noticed how his mother was starting to look more and more worn, as if the toll of the last few difficult years were beginning to show on her face as wrinkles around her eyes and forehead. She had always been a beautiful woman, Joslyn mused, but now her beauty was starting to fade, as if the constant strain and anxiety had caused her to age prematurely.

Abbe had also lost some of her lightness of spirit, although she still was a "force of energy" as her mother called her. That energy had now become more contained and somber, as if it was being harnessed to fight some of the unfamiliar and unexpected challenges the Q'ehazi world had faced recently.

Joslyn was eager to talk about his experience with the strange man in his clinic, and he was uncharacteristically voluble, as the others questioned him about what had happened. He showed his fellow diners the small metal object from the "gun" that the man had described.

"You're saying this thing was *inside* his leg?" Abbe puzzled incredulously, holding the object between thumb and forefinger and squinting at it to see it more clearly. All of their communication was done in thought-words since they were sitting close together at the dinner table.

"Yes, it was deep in his flesh, I had to dig it out with a knife."

"Ooh, ouch," Abbe winced in empathy.

"I offered him my *Pukatl* herbal tea to help with the pain, but he refused it."

"Too proud," replied Abbe, nodding.

"Was it an accident?" Aurora pursed her lips and shook her head slowly. "That is why we don't have weapons here in Q'ehazi. We don't need to be causing pain to each other."

Aurora pondered for a moment and then remarked, "I think this man also visited me. I remember him, but I hadn't seen him in a long time. I believe he separated from his wife a few months ago. I could divine that there was some agenda behind his visit, as he asked many questions, but I wasn't sure what his agenda was."

"Do you think Barylos sent him?" asked Abbe.

"I cannot tell for sure, but he certainly seemed in distress of an emotional nature like an animal who has been wounded."

"I am glad we have no such thing as weapons," Abbe concluded.

"I agree," Joslyn considered. "Their ways are not ours." He paused for a moment, hesitating over making his next remark. "Perhaps sending Barylos and her people away wasn't the best idea."

"Why do you say that?" responded Aurora with curiosity.

"Excommunicating them has made them angrier and more hostile. Perhaps we should have tried to win them over like we usually do with people who don't understand our ways."

"We *tried* to win them over" retorted Abbe, "and it was impossible."

"Barylos would have been angry no matter what. She has been angry ever since Maudina died," deliberated Aurora. "These are not people who don't *understand* our ways. Barylos was brought up with you and Abbe, she understands our ways perfectly well, she just rejects them, as she rejects everything about our society." Aurora seemed downcast as she made this last comment.

Joslyn remembered how difficult it had been for his mother to send away one of her daughters, and how she had confided in him that the decision kept her up at night and caused her a heartache she had never known before. Even though Barylos had always been "difficult" and obstinate in her own way, a daughter was a daughter, and Aurora was mindful of the fact that excommunication of family members might be looked on poorly by other Q'ehazi. Yet the dangers posed by allowing Barylos to remain free to continue her plans for establishing a new type of governance for all the people of Q'ehazi were too great to be allowed, and so banishment seemed the only option open to her.

For a few moments, the diners continued to eat without communicating. Joslyn turned and smiled at Serano—the quiet and stoical dark-skinned man who was always present and tolerant of others without expressing an opinion of his own—and thought how much they were alike and yet different. Joslyn admired his father's quiet strength of character, yet sometimes she felt that his reticence bordered too much on passivity. In contrast, Abbe had inherited her mother's forceful nature, while also imbuing it with her own very special brand of sunny optimism. Joslyn had always been more like his father, and yet he also had a quiet strength that sometimes veered more toward stubbornness and single-mindedness of purpose. The latter was what had helped him be successful in his career, yet perhaps it also made it more difficult for him to find a woman who would be a good match.

The evening was drawing down to dusk. Joslyn always loved this time of day best, especially when he was eating dinner with his family and chewing over the events of the day as he chewed his food. This time, though, a tinge of danger and sadness hung in the air and marred his mood.

"Did you find out where Barylos is?" Aurora suddenly inquired, fixing her piercing brown eyes on her son for a moment.

"Not precisely, but I know it's somewhere a long way away, and it's in the north across the isthmus path. The man mentioned that he'd had a long journey to reach me, and they were cold at night. It seems they don't have any healers there, which is why he had to travel so far to see me. He says they've constructed dwellings to stay in rather than sleeping in hammocks, so somewhere the temperature isn't controlled, I'd guess."

"Poor things," Abbe responded as a reflex.

Aurora smiled at her daughter. "Always empathetic, my dear. But remember, these people have chosen their life. They *wanted* to live outside of Q'ehazi."

"You keep calling him 'the man.' Don't you even know his name?" asked Abbe.

"He wouldn't tell me. He was pretty secretive," responded Joslyn.

"I wish we knew more about Barylos' plans" his mother mused.

"Well, I did find out that they have weapons, and they are amassing more weapons. Perhaps they are planning to attack us with them, I don't know. The man seemed proud of himself, and he couldn't help boasting about that."

The noise of the meal was dying down, and servers were clearing away dishes to be cleaned. Abbe and Aurora thanked their fellow Q'ehazi. The diners adjourned to a clearing in the forest, where they sat on the ground in a circle around a cheerfully blazing fire. Little fireflies punctured the air with their siren glow, appearing like magical sparkles of light that danced like the flames emanating from the fire. The logs and twigs on the fire crackled, and the smell of wood smoke rose into the air, perfuming the environment. A colorful sunset of blazing gold and pink gave to the dusk of the evening, and the noise of cicadas and tree frogs was beginning its nightly chorus.

Aurora gave a long and despondent sigh. "This situation is challenging for all the Q'ehazi. I don't know what Barylos is planning, but I feel sure she's planning something and she means to disrupt our way of life. I need to do something, but I'm not sure what. I wish I had an answer. It seems as if I've pondered this for months, gone over and over it in my mind, but a solution never comes to me."

Joslyn reflected on how he had not seen his mother run out of ideas before. It was as if this situation was so unfamiliar that it taxed all her normal ways of responding to challenges, and drained her of the vitality needed to come up with new solutions.

Abbe, however, could always be relied upon to think outside the box. Although the years and challenges had tempered her natural exuberance, she still retained her infectious almost childlike enthusiasm and positivity. She rose to her feet and clasped her hands in front of her in an attitude of delighted accomplishment. A beaming smile lit up her face and her black curls bounced in excitement, as she exclaimed suddenly and aloud, "What about Charli? Do you remember her?"

Aurora and Joslyn gazed at her with questioning faces. Joslyn's heart skipped a beat. It had been a long time since he had even thought about the girl from another world. Whenever he did think about her, it was with a twinge of sadness and regret. They had known each other so briefly, and yet she'd had a powerful effect on him. The girl was so young and yet so wise. Although he didn't consciously admit it to himself perhaps meeting Charli was the reason he hadn't settled down with a partner. So, he was still single at the age of 24 when many of his peers were getting married and starting a family of their own.

Aurora smiled, partly at her daughter's elation and partly at the memory of the girl she'd known five years earlier. "Yes, I remember her, of course. But how can she help us?"

"In Charli's world, they have things like guns and weapons, she told me."

"You don't want to bring more of those things here, do you?"

"No, no, of course not. But she might know what to do. Perhaps they have a way of dismantling the guns and weapons. We don't know how to do that because we've never encountered them before. As they have had those things for centuries, surely they have developed some way of protecting themselves."

Aurora nodded. "You could be right. But how are we to contact Charli? Don't you remember, we tried the thought communication before and it didn't work?"

Joslyn agreed and reflected despondently, "Yes, after she left, I tried many times to contact her through dreams, and it never worked."

"I've got an idea," pronounced Abbe with a smile, "I can cross over into her world just briefly."

"But do you know where it is? Maudina went with Charli before and she's no longer with us."

"I went with Charli, too, one time, and she showed me how to get into her world."

"You didn't tell us that!" blurted Joslyn. He felt protective toward his sister, and he didn't like to think of her taking risks, especially without telling anyone. "Wasn't that dangerous?"

"That's why I didn't tell you," Abbe responded with a grin, "I knew you'd worry."

Serano interjected suddenly, breaking his usual silence, "So you crossed over into the other world before? What happened?"

"The air made me sick like with the stones. I couldn't breathe. I only stayed there a few moments."

"And you want to go back?" questioned Joslyn, a plaintive look on his face.

"I'll be all right if I wear a face covering like we all did during the *sickness*. I won't stay too long."

"What will you do there?" asked Aurora.

"I will take one of our ruby stones and bury it beneath the Redbud Tree. That's where Charli first found the shawl, so she knows that place."

"She also needs to have something from Q'ehazi in order to get back," said Joslyn, completing her thought.

"Exactly. Perhaps she's been trying to get back this whole time and couldn't because she didn't have anything in her world to help transport her here."

"So, you will take her an object that can help her to cross the portal," concluded Serano.

"Yes, Abbe, it's a brilliant notion," Aurora agreed.

"Well, as long as you stay safe, and you don't stay too long."

"I promise, big brother."

"You can go. Perhaps it can work," said Joslyn, giving his sister a hug. "Well done, little sister. It's a genius idea."

Chapter Two

The familiar mountains came into view over the horizon, and Charli felt a little surge of happiness at seeing them. It had been too long since she'd seen "her" mountains, as she thought of them. She surprised herself by falling in love with this place that she despised so much at first, the mountains of Western North Carolina and the little town of Weaverton where she and her mother moved from California all those years ago.

Charli enjoyed driving alone and the way it let her mind drift to whatever subject it pleased. She felt a twinge of enthusiasm mingled with trepidation at the realization that it was almost the five-year anniversary of that fateful day. She would be returning to the place of her annual pilgrimage, even though she was expecting yet another disappointment because that's what she did every year. Charli protected herself against this disappointment by anticipating it with a sort of pre-ordained hopelessness and saying things to herself such as, "There's no way I'll find it this year. I never do, so why would this year be any different?"

Yet the little bird of hope fluttered at her heart and said, "Maybe this year will be different, and it is five years after all. That's half a decade since I first discovered it, and surely something has to happen eventually. I mean I can't spend the rest of my life wishing and hoping in vain."

Alternating between hopeful and hopeless, Charli returned once again to the Redbud Tree on her birthday, just as she had done since her 16th birthday five years ago when she found the world of the Q'ehazi for the first time.

Although Charli had lost all means of returning—the shawl was gone, the book had disintegrated to dust, and the rock had gradually dissolved—she still clung to a shred of belief that perhaps the *Pukatl* plant (now grown into a towering tree) was the key to opening the doorway and allowing her to cross the portal. Every year, she carried the plant over to the creek and held it in the air (which became increasingly difficult as the plant grew taller) while she prayed and tried to will the divide between worlds to open again, but it never did.

Instead, the empty air space where the opening should be seemed to mock Charli every year. She walked home despondent and tried to hide her dejection from her mother, not wanting to invoke any questions, and then she placed the *Pukatl* plant by a large window that protected it from the toxic air.

The roads were relatively clear of traffic, which made the journey easier, just one freeway all the way from Raleigh to Asheton before turning north for a few miles to Weaverton. Charli put on her playlist from the iPad connected to Bluetooth and listened to one of her favorite songs, a song she used to enjoy with Nick.

Thinking of Nick brought back all of the anger at him for being such a narcissistic asshole, anger at the friends who sided with him over her after their break-up, and mostly anger at herself for being so stupid as to get involved with him in the first place. How had she managed to choose a man like that, a man almost exactly like the sort of abusive, toxic idiots her mother Angela hooked up with (the last one was Sean), before she had gotten wise enough to make better choices post therapy.

A new thought entered Charli's mind, an appreciation that her mother really had changed for the better after her crisis with Sean. That situation was so bad, it became the wake-up call for Angela, and it enabled her to recognize how she was sabotaging herself with her bad choices. She finally started to make better ones. It also meant she'd chosen to be on her own for a few years while waiting for a decent guy to show up. Charli recognized that her mother had shown real courage by altering her patterns and not settling for any man she knew was wrong for her.

Charli had moderated her concepts about her mother as she watched her grow in independence and strength until she finally found a decent and honorable man to be with, a man who didn't abuse her, and who valued her for who she was. Charli still believed her father was the best man her mother had ever known, and his death was a tragedy for everybody, yet she was aware that this new man, Bill, was a really good man and good for her mother, too.

So how did Charli, who was supposed to be stronger and wiser and more mature than her mother, make the exact same foolish choices?

Charli gave an audible sigh of disapproval as she reflected on those choices. Had she learned nothing from her mother's mistakes and so unconsciously repeated them?

She impulsively turned off the song because it reminded her of Nick too much, and she was done with thinking about him, done with crying, done with soul-searching, done, done, done with all the self-indulgent despair.

Then she made a conscious effort to return to the present moment by gazing through the car window at the scenery around her. She loved this time of year, which also happily coincided with her birthday. The winter was over, the leaves were back on the trees, and the blossoms were just starting to bloom. Green was all around in various shades interspersed with the dogwoods' white and pink blossoms, the Redbud Tree's pink blossoms, and the sky's soft blue with hazy white clouds. The scene was very peaceful after the bustle of Raleigh to which Charli was accustomed. Although she loved being at college, she missed the calmness of her life back home.

Charli vowed to think about only positive things for the rest of her journey. She reflected on the good things about her life now, and how far she had come in 21 years. She'd gone from being an angst-ridden teenager to a confident and mature young adult. Her fierce intelligence and academic ability had won her a scholarship to a good university, and after graduating with a 4.0 GPA, she continued to gain credentials by studying for a master's degree in psychology in order to fulfill her dream of becoming a clinical psychologist.

Charli's ideas about being a medical doctor had changed as she realized her passion for helping people who were suffering from mental and emotional difficulties. She had a vision of offering support to women who suffered domestic abuse and violence, and she knew this was possibly because of her mother's relationship with Sean and how that had affected her. Charli had witnessed many acts of violence and verbal abuse toward her mother, and as a young teen she had felt so powerless to protect Angela or alter the situation. So now she wanted to use her passion to help other women who were in the same boat.

Charli wondered briefly about what had become of Sean after all this time. She hadn't seen him since that day five years ago when she helped him get to the hospital after he became sick. Sean had disappeared from the lives of her mother and herself. Charli didn't even know if he and her mother had communicated after his hospital stay. Oddly enough, Charli and Angela never talked about Sean after that, and he became a taboo subject between them—the elephant in the room that was never discussed. Perhaps there was a tacit agreement to just let bygones be bygones, and Charli was grateful to never have to see him again.

Sean was exactly the reason why she had been expelled from Q'ehazi, and Charli still hated him and would always hate him. He had destroyed the idyllic perfect life that she could have had, and he didn't even care. If she hadn't been followed into Q'ehazi by Sean, perhaps she'd be with Joslyn right now.

Charli felt a lonely tear fall down her cheek at the thought of Joslyn, the handsome dark-skinned young man she had known so briefly five years ago. At 16, she didn't even know what love was, but she thought it might be what she felt for him. He was so unique and special, and Charli didn't think she would ever meet anybody else quite like him. In fact, she felt convinced that nobody like him could possibly exist in her world.

Oh, damn, she was thinking about negative things again, and she'd sworn not to do that! She was becoming her mother in more ways than one.

Charli pulled her mind back to all the good things in her life. She had a successful career on the horizon, good friends, and a great relationship with her mother. She wasn't rich, but by working on holidays she'd managed to support herself throughout her student years, and she knew that once she graduated with her PhD credential and became a licensed psychologist, she could command a decent salary. She also liked where she lived and how she had settled very well into North Carolina.

Tomorrow would be her birthday, and this would give her another chance to make her annual pilgrimage to the Redbud Tree, and to hope for another possibility that the world of Q'ehazi was not forever lost to her.

There was a time when Manteen and his wife Denala shared everything, including friends, possessions, and attitudes toward life in the Q'ehazi society to which they both belonged. He couldn't quite remember when their rift had started. Maybe it was when Denala's cousin came to them begging to be taken in after she was severely injured in an accident and could no longer work or provide for her two young children after her husband perished. Denala offered all of them her hospitality, saying they could stay as long as they wished and share all their meals. She even offered to help with raising the children since her boy and girl were grown and taking care of themselves.

Manteen saw this situation differently. He argued that Denala's cousin should get help from her own village and not from them. He secretly hated the idea of having his private life disrupted by constantly "entertaining" other people he didn't know well. He tended toward a solitary disposition and enjoyed long periods of quiet reflection when he wasn't tending to his vegetable garden. Denala was more social and loved interacting with her cousin, chattering with her about matters close to her heart, and playing games with the children. She argued that it was the "Q'ehazi way" to provide for unexpected guests and to share whatever they had with people who had fallen on hard times.

The situation led to many arguments between them that grew increasingly tense and heated, until eventually Denala's cousin felt unwelcome, moved back to her village with her children, and started a new life. Manteen was incredibly relieved to see her go and believed that all his troubles were over, but unfortunately Denala's resentment persisted, and their relationship was indelibly altered from that time onward.

Their arguments continued, but they were more about the ways they didn't see eye to eye. Manteen loved hunting "just for the sake of it" Denala said, and he had to admit there was a certain thrill to bringing down a deer with his bow and arrow, even if he didn't need to kill it for food. Denala accused him of being a "curmudgeon" and a continual "complainer" and Manteen wondered why that made him a bad person since, in his opinion, there were so many issues to complain about.

When the *sickness* overtook their village, their troubles intensified. They faced an actual challenge at a time when many people had to change their daily routine in order to cope. Denala followed Sovereign Aurora's recommendations scrupulously, making sure to use all of the preventive measures to keep her immune system strong. She took long rigorous walks every day, spent many hours in creative pursuits such as painting and writing, socialized with friends electronically if she couldn't do it in person, and vigilantly wore a nose-and-mouth mask when around other people.

Manteen, however, was resentful about these new restrictions placed upon them, complained constantly that his life was being negatively impacted "through no fault of my own" blamed everybody else for this new stringent life that they were being forced to live, and refused to wear the mask by claiming that it did not do any good anyway.

The rift between them continued to widen. One day, to Manteen's surprise, his wife told him she wanted a divorce and had put all of his possessions on to the ground outside their small abode. Since the *sickness*, all of the communal buildings had been replaced by small houses for single families in order to reduce human contact.

All of a sudden, Manteen was forced to find somewhere else to live. He did this while telling himself "he was tired of all the arguments anyway" and he knew he could grow a vegetable garden anywhere. He moved to the Village of Farmers Southeast, and one day Barylos came and gave a speech that motivated him to join her small band of followers.

He realized in his heart that, although Barylos' words were powerful to him and moved him to act, he would never have decided to join her if Denala had not first thrown him out. But since he was a "free spirit," relatively speaking, with no family to hold him back, he went straight up to Barylos after her speech and announced, "I am ready to join you and your army, if you'll have me." Her stern expression was unwavering as she responded, "Collect your belongings and follow me. Once you join the Liberation Warriors, you can never return home." Manteen nodded in recognition of this commitment and did as she requested. He never looked back from that day forward.

Soon, he was journeying to Barylos' stronghold in the northernmost part of the continent, far from the fringes of Q'ehazi society. His mission to Q'ehazi had been completed, and he had much to tell his leader. He had taken advantage of Joslyn's help in treating his bullet wound, and he even secured the brief conversation with Sovereign Aurora that Barylos had required of him.

Manteen sat on a seat on the moving conveyor belt that all the Q'ehazi used for transportation. This was a wide path moving at a slow speed to make entering and exiting easy. The path followed the contours of the roads that went the length and breadth of the Q'ehazi territory.

Manteen studied the faces of his co-travelers as if they were aliens to him, even though not so long ago, he'd considered himself one of them. It was a Q'ehazi custom to smile politely at others sitting nearby or walking down the aisles, even if they were strangers. But Manteen refused to follow this custom, and he simply glowered at those around him, regarding them with eyes full of hostility and judgment.

He knew that he had done the right thing by joining Barylos and her army of Liberation Warriors. This decision gave him a new sense of purpose. Denala could never understand him or the man he had become. He felt that he was the future, and she was the past. She was a follower, and he was a leader. He didn't get along with all the Q'ehazi "sheep." He was a Liberation Warrior, and he even had a weapon to prove it. He felt powerful and invincible. For the first time in his life, he was understood by the other members of his group, he was appreciated, and he belonged.

Chapter Three

Abbe had not made this journey in five years, and yet she seemed to remember the way quite clearly. In the past, she had always relished being outdoors and took a sensuous enjoyment in the sights and sounds of nature. But these days she was too distracted and concerned about the future to focus on the present. Her mood was increasingly gloomy in the past few years, with all of the challenges the Q'ehazi world faced, and she felt her innocence had been stripped away from her quite suddenly, forcing her to confront the reality that not everybody was as prepared to live together harmoniously as she had once believed.

The death of her Aunt Maudina hit Abbe very hard, as she had been a shining light to all her nieces and nephews, as well as to her students at the Creative Arts and Dreaming school. Although Barylos was also devastated by the loss of her favorite relative, her reaction was more toward anger than sadness at what she perceived to be the injustice of it all. In contrast, Abbe's grief was pure and simple, just grief at the loss of a person whose optimism and positive spirit she valued and emulated.

After the *sickness* had taken hold of the populace shortly after Sean's expulsion, many of the familiar societal norms shifted out of necessity, and this made everything harder and colder that had once seemed warm and inviting. People were no longer expected to do everything together no matter what. The sick people were isolated as if they were lepers because their disease made them so contagious that they could quickly infect those around them. The healthy people started to build enclosures for these sick people in order to contain them and their sickness, and that was also contrary to the usual Q'ehazi way of life that was all out in the open and the fresh air.

Although Sovereign Aurora advocated for more preventive methods to bolster people's immune systems—eating healthily and exercising and fighting the virus by keeping one's body strong—even she recognized that not every person could be saved this way. Some people were just not physically strong enough to counteract the *sickness*. So, especially in the early days, many people died, and others were left with permanent physical disabilities.

But even worse than these physical ailments were the lingering emotional and mental effects on the people. That was like a sickness and a much worse unseen virus affecting people in subtle ways that were not at first noticeable, and yet they spread quickly and virulently and attacked their spirits, beliefs, and faith in the goodness of humanity and the value of the Q'ehazi ways of welcoming and offering friendship.

It was astounding to Abbe how quickly a small group of people had banded together and formed an outlying society vehemently opposed to everything the Q'ehazi held dear. This group of mostly males and a few females were followers or supporters of Barylos, who was the major ringleader in the dissent. They called themselves the Liberation Warriors, and they were so aggressive and hostile that Sovereign Aurora excommunicated them, including her daughter, and they began living a long way from the main Q'ehazi villages. Abbe had little knowledge of how they lived, but she knew they had formed their own society and their intentions toward her mother were not at all amicable.

Abbe came upon the little grove of trees by the creek where she remembered seeing the Redbud Tree. She knew what she had to do and steeled herself to do what was required, knowing that it would take strength and courage.

She took a ruby stone from her pocket and looked at it in an effort to imbue it with a special quality that would help her communicate with Charli and inspire her friend to visit the tree again and discover the secret left for her. She took out a small trowel and dug a hole for the stone.

At that moment, she wasn't sure if she could achieve her goal because it had been so long since she'd come here and, at that earlier time, Charli accompanied her. She knew she had to at least try since nothing else successfully communicated with her friend.

Abbe touched the trunk of the tree just as Charli did all those years ago. She felt a faintness and a dizziness come over her, and then she saw the tear appear and hover in the air as it had done before. All of her memories came flooding back instantly, but she didn't stop to remember them because she had an important task to do, and she had to complete it expeditiously.

So, Abbe stepped through the portal into the other world. She remembered to quickly pull a mask over her mouth and nose so that the toxic air could not harm her. Abbe looked around to orient herself to this alternate universe. Everything was muffled, sounds were less sharp, colors were less vibrant, and the air was foggy and dull as if covered by a screen.

Abbe refused to spend time for reflection on these sensations as her visit had to be short, so she began digging a hole for the ruby stone, placed the stone into the hole, and covered it up. She was starting to feel unwell and coughing a little but ignored her discomfort, pushing herself to complete the task and quickly retreat through the portal.

She looked at the small mound and wondered if she should leave any other sign for Charli, something to help her friend find the ruby. Abbe found a small twig and wrote a large "Q" in the ground, hoping that this letter remained until Charli came, *if* Charli came.

Abbe hurried back through the tear, closed it, and started her return home. On the way, she passed by a small grove of trees about a mile from her village that she knew well. She called them the Standing Tall family. Many times she sought guidance from these trees with whom she felt especially connected. As she neared the tree with the largest trunk—the one she called Old Grandfather Tree—she placed her hand on the rough gnarly bark and soaked in the tree's powerful energy.

"You are back, Little Girl," the tree said to Abbe in her mind, and she felt a warm flood of protective energy wash over her.

"I know I've asked you for help before," explained Abbe silently, "but we Q'ehazi need help now. Just as your tree family is sometimes damaged by a virus that destroys your branches and spreads through your roots, so has my Q'ehazi family been attacked by a *sickness* spreading throughout our society and into our very core. We have stayed strong, and even though many people died, many survivors remain, and we have learned ways to ward off the *sickness*, so it doesn't attack us again. During this time, however, some of our people turned away from the Q'ehazi ways, and they are threatening to attack us with their weapons."

Abbe started to cry, as she continued to tell her concerns to her wise old friend. "This has never happened to us and so we are unprepared. Our usual ways of negotiation and bartering are not working with Barylos and her followers. We need new strategies. Our Q'ehazi nature is based on peace and harmony, and we don't wish to lose that and become something other than who we are. How do we maintain our integrity and still battle against this evil that has spread like cancer among our people?"

Abbe listened intently for a message. The Grandfather Tree was connected by his roots to other members of his tree family. These members included three trees with one trunk that Abbe called the Three Sisters, the small sapling standing apart from the others that she called Young Boy, and the Dancing Trees that stood with branches reaching up to the sky in a joyful pose.

Abbe soon received their response, and it didn't surprise her, "Seek guidance from another" said the Grandfather Tree, "another person who is from another world and who can give you a different perspective on your troubles."

Abbe was grateful to receive confirmation that she had to reach out to an old friend—Charli. She didn't know if she would be successful in communicating with her after all this time, but at least she had taken action and done all she could. Now, she had to wait and stay optimistic that help would come.

Chapter Four

Angela was frequently in the kitchen whenever she was waiting for her daughter to come home and visit. Just now, she was making a chicken pot pie to put in the freezer for the next day since Charli wouldn't return until quite late that evening.

Angela reflected on how she was a very different person from who she was just a few years ago before she met Bill. In her pre-Bill days, she was so unsure of herself, always doubting her ability to do things successfully, always taking the blame in relationships, and always believing that everything was her fault.

Time spent on her own for a few years while she worked on her patterns with her therapist had been time very well spent, even though the experience was certainly lonely and unfamiliar. On many occasions, Angela even missed Sean—Sean of all people! Angela's therapist explained that a "trauma bond" made her feel so connected to Sean, and that made it so difficult to release her connection to him, even when she knew he was a bad person who lied to her and the other women in his life.

Bill was a whole different story. When Angela met Bill, it wasn't love at first sight, but she felt comfortable and safe around him. Like a pound cake with no frosting, he was simply a good man who was genuinely interested in her, not for her money or connections, but just because he saw the goodness in her, as well as the strength and the courage that she'd built up in the years she'd been on her own.

Bill got on quite well with Charli, which was amazing because Charli made it her mission to hate every man her mother dated who wasn't her father, Chuck Speranza. It was just impossible to hate Bill, though, because he was genuinely kind and warm and the sort of man who anybody would take a liking to, male or female. Salt of the Earth, as Angela's father had to admit.

Since she hadn't seen Charli for several months while she was away at college in Raleigh, Angela asked Bill not to come over this evening, so she could spend time with her daughter. They needed to reconnect, and Bill understood. He was a little older than Angela, and he had teenage girls of his own from a previous marriage, so he knew all about the special bond that exists between mothers and daughters, how important and precious it was, and how challenging it could be.

Angela was excited about Charli's return, and this time she was not even flustered. On previous occasions, a visit from her daughter had felt rather like a difficult exam she had to pass. But this time, Angela felt a warm and comfortable stability about her house and her life that enabled her to accommodate her daughter without needing the younger woman's validation or approval. Angela told Alexa to play classic rock while she prepared the meal and waited to hear Charli's car through the kitchen window that overlooked the front porch.

Around five o'clock, Angela heard the sound of a vehicle turning into her driveway. Her immediate assumption was that Charli was home earlier than expected, and her heart lifted, as she left her meal preparation in the kitchen to go to the front door in anticipation of her daughter's homecoming, with a welcoming smile on her face. But her smile slowly vanished and was replaced by a puzzled frown like a cloud moving across the sun and darkening the sky.

She recognized the red Toyota in her driveway, not as her daughter's car, but a vehicle with which she was very familiar from years past, and that she had hoped never to see again.

She meant to hide behind the safety of the front door, but it was too late to hide because she recognized the car and its driver as he stepped out of the car after noticing her. His broad smile and expansive gesture of open arms were the exact mirror opposite of what she was expressing, with her furrowed forehead and arms crossed as if to defend herself from an unpredictable onslaught.

"Hey, you must have known I was coming!" Sean half-joked, as he sauntered up to the door. Angela noticed that he was dressed quite nicely in loose, expensive-looking, dark-gray slacks and a short-sleeved polo shirt open at the throat to reveal a tanned chest. Sean no longer sported his trademark five-day stubble and tousled hair, and his clean-shaven face and well-pressed clothes made him look like a car salesman instead of the construction worker that she had previously known.

Angela retreated a couple of steps back into the doorway and closed the door a little, as she saw the unwelcome visitor making his way to her front steps.

"I didn't know. You should have called first. I thought you were Bill coming home." Some protective response prompted Angela to use Bill as the excuse rather than her daughter as she didn't want Sean to know that Charli was expected home at any minute.

If Angela had expected Sean to be put off by her mentioning of another man's name, she was disappointed because he didn't even hesitate. He walked right up to her and planted a kiss on her cheek before she could stop him. Angela recoiled at his touch and shrank even further into the doorway.

Sean appeared a little discomfited by her rebuff, as if he'd expected that a kiss would automatically make this woman his again. "Woah, you're not pleased to see me?"

"Well, it's been a long time," Angela began.

"Sure, it's been a minute. I never stopped thinking about you, though." Sean's face had that demeanor of boyish candor that had made her fall in love with him the first time over five years ago. Angela felt that familiar pang again, only this time she realized how false it was and pushed the feeling away.

"I'm sorry," Angela faltered and was instantly annoyed with herself for starting off with an apology to this man who in the past had done nothing but hurt her and her daughter.

"Can I come in?" Sean almost pleaded, displaying his most winning smile.

"No," Angela replied with more alacrity than she'd expected. She did not want Sean anywhere near this house, especially not when her daughter was coming home at any minute. On any other occasion, she might have been tempted to let him in for old time's sake, but right now he couldn't have shown worse timing. Angela's protective instincts about Charli overpowered any lingering affection she may have felt for her ex-boyfriend.

Sean reflected for a moment then tried another tactic. "So, I've been doing pretty well for myself the past few years living down in Florida. I got my real estate license, and I have been running a business with my brother. I really turned my life around."

"Yes," Angela agreed, "you look well. You really do."

"I'm in town for just a few days, and I thought I'd look you up and that it would be really cool to see you. But if you're too busy…." Sean's words drifted like a balloon slowly deflating.

Angela said nothing, and let her silence be her response.

"So, I guess you got yourself a new guy. True?"

"Yes." Angela felt a little thrill of triumph as she saw the look of disappointment momentarily cloud Sean's face. In the past, she had imagined this moment many times, and now it had come to fruition in reality and her momentary victory tasted sweet.

"Oh well, good for you, I guess." Sean appeared magnanimous, and Angela gave an inward sigh of relief as she watched him turn away and start to leave.

Another thought apparently struck him and he turned back. Taking a small wrapped package from his pocket, he said, "I brought this for Charli. I remembered her birthday is tomorrow."

As he handed the gift to Angela, who felt guilty for rejecting him despite this gracious gesture.

"Thanks. That's sweet of you."

"I guess she's coming home for her birthday. Right?"

Angela nodded, forgetting her earlier impulse to hide from Sean the knowledge of Charli's visit. He smiled and jumped in his car and drove off, giving Angela a cheerful wave goodbye.

Angela had a strange instinct she'd just been tricked into making a mistake. She pushed the feeling away and tossed Sean's gift into the trash before Charli could see it. She was determined to hide her former boyfriend's visit from her daughter and Bill. There was no need to worry either of them with something that was never ever going to happen again.

"So, you finally split up with Nick?" Angela breathed a sigh of relief, and gave her daughter a warm smile of approval.

"Yes. I can't believe it took me so long."

"Was it traumatic?"

"Not really. Actually, I just feel relieved more than anything. It took such a lot of energy dealing with his ass-hole-ry."

Angela laughed. "I'm glad you can still make up words, Honey."

Charli grinned. "Me too. What's for dinner, Mom?" She got up off the couch and started meandering to the kitchen with a glass of wine.

"Oh my God, are you hungry? I thought you'd be too tired."

Charli opened the fridge door and peered inside. "Well, I *am* tired, but that doesn't stop me from being hungry. You know me, growing girl and all that."

"Well, I hope you're not growing any more. You're tall enough already, my girl."

"You're just jealous. Hey, what's this?" Charli inquired, discovering the chicken pot pie covered in foil. "Looks yummy."

"It's supposed to be for tomorrow, but yes you can have some."

Charli tried to spoon some of the dish on to a plate and eat it cold, but her mother stopped her.

"Good heavens, let me heat it up for you. Get back in that living room and I'll bring you a proper plate."

"Okay, Mom. Thanks," Charli sighed and plopped back down on the couch again. In a few minutes, her eyes closed, and she dozed off. She hadn't realized how tired she was after her five-hour drive.

After she got upstairs to her old bedroom late that evening, Charli realized how huge the *Pukatl* tree had grown. The leaves almost protruded from the glass top, and the tree seemed constrained as if it was desperate to escape and become a real mature grown tree in the wilds of nature. Charli recognized with a shock that there was no way she could carry this now fully grown tree to the creek when she made her vigil the next day. She'd have to leave it behind this time, for the first time. She hoped that wasn't a bad omen.

This time, she prayed, maybe *this time* she'd finally return to Q'ehazi. Although in actuality, she'd given up hope and was making this pilgrimage out of habit and a sense of duty. She knew if she didn't do it, she'd castigate herself for her lack of devotion and loyalty. She wanted to prove to herself that she still cared about Q'ehazi enough to make this annual journey and try once more.

She discerned something else about the *Pukatl* tree. Not only was it about six feet tall, and taller than Charli, but it seemed to be sprouting some interesting looking fruit from the end of the branches. They were about the size of a kiwi fruit and orange-red with smooth glossy peel. Charli remembered seeing these fruits before when they had been taken off the tree and eaten by the Q'ehazi people. She even remembered the taste of the fruit when it was ripe enough to eat, a slightly bitter, slightly nutty taste, like a cross between an apple and a walnut, as she'd described it to herself then. Not overly sweet and certainly not unpleasant.

This was the first time Charli had seen actual fruit on the tree, although she had seen small pods that maybe were the genesis of the fruit. She selected the largest one hanging close to the bottom of the tree and gently pulled on it. To her surprise, it came off quite easily in her hand, and she gave a little gasp of shock and delight. She gazed at the fruit, as if it were a magical object capable of transporting her to an alternate universe. Then a new idea came to her. Perhaps this was the key to her entry back into Q'ehazi—not the whole tree this time, but the fruit of the tree that had grown in this world and this climate without perishing, yet still contained whatever power it had that could provide a portal into the other world she had cherished for such a long while.

Charli remembered that the main medicinal ingredient of the plant was contained in the leaves, and they had to be ground down and processed in order to achieve their full healing power. She felt animated at the idea that perhaps she could finally create some of this medicine for use in her world, too. Even though she was no longer going to be a doctor, Charli still wished to be of use in her world, and she liked the idea of having a "discovery" that nobody else in her world had known about before she introduced it. She remembered all the positive effects that regular use of this herb had on the Q'ehazi people over the centuries, and she hoped to introduce it into her world with similar results.

With a smile slowly spreading across her face at the knowledge of what she had discovered, Charli carefully placed the precious object on her bedside table, then turned out the light and lay down on her bed. In a few moments, exhaustion overcame her and she descended into a deep slumber.

Chapter Five

The coyotes yapping outside the window woke her on an unseasonably warm evening for late April. She'd left the window open, so the din was quite loud. Charli lay there listening for a few moments, then got up and peered outside. The coyotes were gone as she did not see them. So, she closed the window, fell back into bed, and willed herself to go back to sleep.

Then she remembered her dream—fragments of it, anyway. Something about Q'ehazi, she was trying to get back. Something about reincarnation. Who was it? Somebody she wanted to meet again.

Charli tried to bring the wisps of memory back to her again, but the drowsiness overcame her before she could bring any more back into her consciousness.

The next thing she knew, she was back in the same dream. Except that this time, she knew she was in a dream. A lucid dream!

Something was coming toward her: a coyote growling this time rather than yapping, its teeth bared. It didn't look at all friendly. In fact, its eyes were glowing red like a werewolf in a horror movie. Charli backed away slowly, keeping her eyes on the wolf for that was what it was now.

Suddenly, she remembered that she was in a dream and that she had total power over what happened to her. She imagined herself floating up and into the air, and then that was what she was doing. She rose higher and higher, and she was flying over the ground, and the wolf had disappeared. Charli enjoyed the sensation of flying.

Charli woke up with a gasp of shock and opened her eyes suddenly. At first, she wasn't quite sure where she was. In her dorm at college? In her old house in California? Oh yes, she was here in her bedroom in Weaverton, NC, with her mother. Gradually, her breathing became regular, and her heartbeat slowed.

The dream she'd been having was very vivid, so much so that she could recall it in great detail. Charli remembered how the Q'ehazi people regularly wrote down all their dreams and analyzed them later; in fact, that was the purpose of Maudina's Dream Academy. Charli had never bothered to transcribe a dream before, but this time that was all she wanted to do quickly before it faded. So, she got out her tablet and wrote on the scratch pad all the details of her dream.

Charli looked at her watch to see what time it was and what the weather would be like that day. The hour was just after 7:00 a.m. Charli hadn't expected to wake up so early, especially as it was her birthday today and there was no work or school. But since she was awake, she decided she may as well look at her social media pages to see who had sent her birthday wishes.

Charli had long ago given up the childish game of competing with friends to see who got the most "likes" and birthday wishes. Still, she did enjoy hearing from people she hadn't spoken to in a while and touching base with them.

Charli smiled as she saw the various birthday greetings and well wishes from friends and family. She felt a mixture of relief and disappointment that there was zero communication from Nick. He wouldn't have forgotten, so he was probably punishing her by pretending her birthday meant nothing to him anymore. Well, screw him. She didn't want to hear from him anyway as it would just complicate things.

Shashawna had sent her a funny video the day before since her time zone was different and she didn't want to be late. Knowing how much Charli loved animals, the video was a montage of funny moments captured on a wildlife cam, and Charli laughed out loud at their antics.

There was also a name Charli didn't recognize at first because it had been so long since she'd communicated with this person. It was her old teacher from fifth grade in California, Ms. Battaglia. The kids called her "Batty Batshit" because of her flamboyant way of dressing and her eccentric behavior. But Charli secretly admired her and preferred her to the other teachers with their bland conventional ways. In fact, Ms. Battaglia was the only teacher at that school who had seen something special about Charli and had seemed to favor her, always giving her an 'A' for her papers. Ms. Battaglia taught art and history, and she reminded Charli a little of Maudina in the Q'ehazi world. Even though Charli had never actually attended the Art Retreat to which she'd been invited a couple of years later by her teacher in North Carolina, the fact that a hastily drawn picture had won her this opportunity had given her confidence in her artistic abilities that had first been noticed by Ms. Battaglia.

For the first time in many years, Ms. Battaglia had sent Charli a happy birthday wish. Seeing the face of her teacher that she hadn't seen in so long prompted Charli to think about sharing her dream with her. Charli couldn't understand what the dream was trying to tell her—if anything. If anybody knew what the dream clues were meant to reveal, it would be old Batty Batshit.

So, Charli sent her a Facebook message not really expecting a reply. To her surprise, the response came right back. Apparently, Ms. Battaglia had also left California and was living in Maine with her husband having retired from teaching some years back.

Charli felt a twinge of guilt at the discovery that Ms. Battaglia was married. They had all assumed she was a batty old spinster. After all, who would be crazy enough to marry her? But actually, she might have been quite pretty in her youth, with her flowing gray hair that may once have been red, and her tall stately figure still vigorous for her age.

Charli was happy that Ms. Battaglia didn't think she was crazy, even to ask about the dream. She was glad to find someone she could talk to about it, as her mother wouldn't have understood anything. Charli had still not mentioned the world of Q'ehazi to anybody. Since she had not seen Sean since he'd left town after breaking up with her mother, she imagined he was the only other person who knew about the other world. Hopefully, he was too embarrassed about how he'd been thrown out of there to talk about the world with other people, and he was probably just trying to forget the whole thing.

Charli also felt affection for Ms. Battaglia because she had given her Casper when he was just a little kitten. He came from a litter that Ms. Battaglia's cat had given birth to, and he was the last one to be adopted.

Ms. Battaglia had not forgotten about Casper, and she asked after him, so Charli had to admit sadly that he had died and she did not have the heart to replace him with another cat.

Ms. Battaglia also said something that Charli found interesting and, in fact, rather amazing. She said that Casper was meant to lead Charli to something or somewhere. Also, that there was a sign, and Charli would recognize it, so she must "go back" to the last place she'd seen Casper.

Well, that, of course, was the Redbud Tree where Charli had originally buried her cat after he'd been run over, on her birthday now five years ago. She had not mentioned the discovery of the Q'ehazi world, or anything about her adventures there, to Ms. Battaglia, so it was extraordinary that her former teacher gave her this instruction seemingly out of the blue.

It was even more evident that Charli had to go back to the Redbud Tree and look again for the portal, this time with the aid of the fruit she had inadvertently grown. She didn't know what would transpire, but she knew she had to go back.

Chapter Six

So, she was here again at the Redbud Tree. It looked old and worn to her now. She stroked the bark with her fingers, and it felt prickly and hard. She inhaled the air that was fresh and clean after the rainstorm the previous day. She recalled how in Q'ehazi the rain came predictably every day at 3: p.m. without fail because they had created it that way. Yet here in Weaverton where the climate wasn't controlled, it still rained, but in an unpredictable fashion. The only thing predictable about the rain was that it would happen, it would be warm at this time of year, and it wouldn't last long.

Charli had a strange sort of confidence, a faith that whatever was meant to happen would happen, and that now was the right time.

Charli considered herself "spiritual not religious". She didn't accompany her mother to church, but she did believe in a "higher power", and not just because she'd learned about it in rehab as a teenager, but because she knew in her heart there was something other, and something greater than herself, although she wasn't sure how it was operated or even if it could be called God. Some of her friends—fellow addicts who'd gotten sober—hated all the AA references to "religious shit", which they felt was a turnoff, but Charli enjoyed the idea of "surrendering to a higher power", as she recognized that it gave her life some structure in an otherwise chaotic and unruly world.

Being in nature as she was now always enabled Charli to reflect on things more easily, which was one of the reasons why she liked to come home and spend time in the mountains again. Her life in Raleigh didn't include a lot of time for soul-searching or reflection, as it was filled with social activities and academic or career goals that needed to be achieved. There, her brain was constantly active and striving for something. Here, that activity was turned off, and it was relieving to "just be" for a few moments.

Charli regarded this place by the creek and the Redbud Tree as her sacred, special place, ever since the first time when she had discovered the portal here, the portal into another world, a world she had loved and respected and that she had longed to get back to for half a decade. The longing to get back to Q'ehazi was even stronger now, as she was so close to the portal that had existed before, and she listened to the sounds of bird songs and the nearby rushing of water in the creek. The longing was like an ache in her chest, very similar to that feeling you get when you're "in love" and you ache to see the sight of your beloved, just to catch a glimpse of their face or hear their voice.

Thinking of love, Charli remembered how it had felt the first time she saw Joslyn. He was introduced to her as her friend's brother, but there was something more than that, some recognition they had a connection that went deeper. At least, that was how Charli perceived it, although she had no idea if he had perceived it the same way. Perhaps he had forgotten all about her by now, as it had been so long after all, and they had both been teenagers. Now, he was probably married to a "nice Q'ehazi girl", with a couple of kids who were being raised by the village in true Q'ehazi fashion, going to the outdoor school with their peers, sleeping in their comfortable hammocks at night, visiting with extended family members in the longhouse on occasion, singing their own songs, and talking about their dreams.

Charli recalled everything that had happened to her in Q'ehazi as vividly as if it were yesterday, as if it were painted on her brain in bright colors that wouldn't fade. Charli heard about how traumatic memories haunt one's mind and cannot be "filed away" appropriately in the subconscious mind because they stay present in the conscious mind. She wondered if beautiful and exceptional memories also acted in this way. Her memories of Q'ehazi were so much clearer and more present than memories of anything else that had happened to her in her young life.

Charli felt a little shiver run through her, as a gust of wind blew her hair to the side, and she realized that the day was progressing, it was already mid-afternoon, the sky was darkening as if to warn of an impending rainstorm, and she needed to act quickly if she was going to complete her goal of making it back into Q'ehazi.

Unsure what to do in the moment, Charli held the fruit she'd brought and closed her eyes, willing something to happen, though she wasn't sure what that might be. She stayed that way for a few minutes, but there was no change in her environment. So, she tried hugging the tree, placing her head to one side on its trunk and allowing the scent of the bark to spread over her. Although this was somewhat comforting, it still didn't produce any results. So, she walked all around the tree, while talking to it aloud, asking it to "please let me go to Q'ehazi" over and over (feeling rather silly and hoping nobody else would come along and discover her doing this unusual activity). All this exercise was starting to make her feel warmer, so she put the fruit back in her pocket, took off her jacket, and put it on the ground beside the tree.

As she walked around the tree, she noticed that she kept stumbling over a small bump in the ground every time she passed by a certain spot. As she looked down, she saw that the bump was the only place that was not covered by the usual leaves and pine needles that tended to fall in November every year. The ground also felt harder as if the soil was more compacted there.

So, she knelt down to investigate. Yes, there was definitely a small mound. Charli wondered, *Had it been there before?* Of course, she hadn't examined the ground so closely the previous times she went to the Redbud Tree, and she hadn't walked around the tree before either. She still had a feeling something was new.

The rain the previous evening had left the ground quite moist, so any evidence of a symbol or marking in the ground had been washed away. Nevertheless, the small mound was intriguing enough to motivate Charli to investigate it further.

Charli started to pull away the dirt with her fingers, remembering an earlier time when she'd buried her cat here and had to dig with her spade for some time. Because the soil was damp, it was easier to dislodge. There were no tree roots or stones to get in her way, which was another sign that this was a mound that had been created and was not a natural phenomenon. So, Charli kept tearing away at the earth with her hands until a few inches of soil had been uncovered.

There were times when Charli hesitated, wondering if she was crazy to keep digging. Perhaps it was simply the strength of her desire that was causing her to see this small mound of soil as something significant. She remembered watching a documentary on TV about an archeological dig, and the fantastic excitement of the diggers when they discovered something apparently unremarkable that was a "huge discovery" to them. A kind of obsession drove her on. She kept telling herself, *Just a little more, and maybe I'll find something. Just a little more.*

Then she saw something that gave her a jolt of recognition and potential joy crept into her heart. *Had this been here before?* She didn't know. *Was it something that had been here all along or recently placed?*

Charli sat back for a minute and exhaled partly due to shock and partly as preparation for the next step. What she saw was a bright red glint of color in the soil from some object buried just beneath the surface.

Now galvanized into action, Charli continued digging until she had unearthed the object sufficiently to see what it was: a bright red ruby stone very similar to the one she remembered from years ago, the one that Sean stole from the Honor Circle.

Charli clawed at the soil feverishly until she completely dislodged the stone and then she held it up. It was about the size of an apple, hard and shiny to the touch. The stone was covered in moist soil, so Charli held it up to the sunlight as she brushed off as much soil as she could with her fingers.

At this moment, Charli heard a rustling of leaves behind her, and she turned quickly to see the one person she least wished to see standing a few feet from her.

Although Angela told Sean, in no uncertain terms, that he was not welcome in her house, he had managed to glean that her daughter was returning home for her annual birthday visit. He was also smart enough to predict that her visit would include the pilgrimage to the Redbud Tree. He followed her as he had done five years earlier and managed to remain hidden long enough to see all of Charli's perambulations around the tree and her subsequent discovery of the red ruby stone, which to his great delight and surprise was what he coveted more than anything. He emerged from his hiding place, ready to do battle and claim his rightful prize.

It took only a few moments for the two adversaries to lock eyes before Sean pounced on Charli and wrestled her to the ground. He had no compunctions about harming a woman, and he was strong enough to incapacitate her for a few seconds, which was long enough for him to grab the ruby stone and thrust it in his pocket.

The few seconds it took for Sean to zip up his pocket gave Charli just enough time to scramble to her feet and push him from behind to unbalance him so that he'd drop the stone. Unfortunately, since she was smaller and weaker than him, her efforts were in vain, and he was unbalanced only momentarily, which was not enough time to harm him.

Sean choked back a laugh as he regained his balance and staggered toward the nearby creek.

"Don't you try any of your tricks on me now, girl," he warned.

"Give it back! Give it back!" she yelled after Sean. "You bastard! That doesn't belong to you. Give it back!"

Charli's rage overcame any fear about a man she knew to be dangerous, and she followed him as quickly as she could, while continuing to hurl invectives at his retreating back.

Sean was more intent on getting away with the stone than on disempowering this girl, so he ignored Charli's remonstrations and pushed through the trees to the creek. His intention was to wade through the shallow waters of the creek in his heavy rubber boots, knowing that it would be more difficult for Charli to follow him. On the other side of the creek was a steep muddy bank and then a fence around the neighboring horse property. Sean felt certain he could straddle the five-foot fence with the stone hidden safely inside his pocket.

Sean had correctly guessed that his progress would be faster than Charli's, as she hesitated at the edge of the creek, unwilling to encounter icy cold waters and sharp rocks in her soft cloth sneakers. What he hadn't bargained for, however, was the presence of a blue line hovering in the air that could represent a tear in the universe and a portal to an alternate world. It was similar to the brown line that both he and Charli had used to enter the world of Q'ehazi five years ago, the only difference being the color and the location.

At first, Charli couldn't understand why the man she was pursuing suddenly stopped and stood motionless in the middle of the creek, seeming undeterred by the icy waters rushing past him. She thought he'd changed his mind and decided to return the stone. He actually turned briefly to face her and gave her a mysterious and triumphant grin, as if he'd made some miraculous discovery. Then in a reversal of the exact situation five years earlier, to Charli's amazement, he stepped forward and literally vanished.

Charli might have been more surprised if she hadn't done the same thing when she discovered the Q'ehazi. After the initial momentary shock, she ignored any temporary discomfort, and hastily splashed into the creek, sneakers and all, in hot pursuit of the man who had obviously entered the other world. Her intense emotions of anger and fear were the motivating forces urging her on, and she sloshed through the water without heeding where she was going.

Charli heard the sounds of the rushing creek, which seemed much louder now that she was in the water, and she felt the icy cold of the stream. She swayed and staggered, trying to retain her balance among the rocks as she made it to the line.

As she had done five years ago, she stretched out her hand and touched the blue line. It felt raspy beneath her fingers, and she drew apart the edges of the tear to reveal the other world. She was so excited, so intent on following Sean, and so sure that she had found Q'ehazi again that she didn't even look much at what was beyond the tear. She barreled straight through it, as soon as she had opened it wide enough to get through. She had her eyes closed in glorious anticipation of what she would experience on the other side.

She was very grateful that the next thing she felt was a cessation of the icy cold water around her calves, so obviously there was not a creek at this spot in this world. She felt a tingle of anticipation before she opened her eyes, expecting to behold some glorious vision of the Q'ehazi world. But when she opened her eyes…all she could see was blackness.

Literally, just that. Blackness, as if in the vastness of space with no stars or atmosphere, with no sun or moon or light peeking in anywhere.

Charli strained to see something, hoping that eventually her eyes would get used to the blackness and she'd be able to see, but all of her efforts were in vain.

So, she decided to step forward anyway, even though she didn't know what she was stepping into. She was grateful that the cold wetness had gone from around her feet and legs, and she seemed to be stepping on firm ground. She could not see anything, but she could feel that her legs were dry and not so cold. In fact, the air around her was warm, or even hot, and very dry. Charli couldn't see Sean anywhere; in fact, he had completely disappeared.

Chapter Seven

Charli became aware of some sounds around her punctuating the stillness. She continued to walk with great trepidation through the darkness, with her heart beating almost out of her chest and having no idea what was before her.

The ground beneath her seemed solid and flat. There was an odd smell in the air that she was unable to recognize. It reminded her a little of the smell after snuffing out a match, and yet it was much stronger than that and lingering on the air as if a thousand matches had been extinguished all at once. The odor assailed her, and she wrinkled her nose, trying to avoid or expel the smell but it persisted.

The sounds also were jarring and not at all pleasant. Crackling and popping sounds came erratically, sometimes just a few and then a lot. Charli thought of fireworks on July 4 or the backfiring of cars. She realized with a little shock that there were also human sounds, more high-pitched, in the distance but seeming to get louder as if she was walking toward them. Wailing, yelling, screaming…sounded like a lot of people, and the screams and yells were high-pitched, as if coming from women.

Charli kept moving forward, although now she was creeping slowly and with great hesitation. She wished so much that she could at least see something in front of her. *Am I blind in this world? Why is it so pitch black?* Charli was finding it difficult to breathe, and she wasn't sure if this was because of the rising panic in her chest or the stiflingly hot air with that acrid smell.

At last, and to her partial relief, Charli detected a small glimmer of light in front of her. It seemed to be coming from way off in the distance, but at least it gave her hope that something existed she could walk toward, and she could be certain now she wasn't blind, but simply in a very dark environment. She tried looking up into the sky, as she assumed it was nighttime and therefore she should see some stars. But there was no light coming from stars or a moon that she could see. Perhaps there was cloud cover, or perhaps the smell was coming from smoke that permeated the air so densely that no stars were visible.

As Charli moved toward the light, the good news was that it was growing larger the closer she approached it. Charli detected a long line of orange light or lights on the horizon. Perhaps there was a town or some other human habitation that was responsible for the glowing light.

Charli started to wish she hadn't made this hasty decision to wade into the creek and pull apart the divide between worlds. For the first time, she thought, *Perhaps this wasn't Q'ehazi at all but another different world.* She hadn't placed her hands on the Redbud Tree or, in fact, been anywhere near the tree at the time she went through the tear. She hadn't been holding on to the red ruby stone that had been buried under the Redbud Tree by somebody from Q'ehazi in the hopes that she would find it or the *Putkatl* fruit that she'd brought with her on purpose.

Charli felt remorse for her impulsive actions. After five years of waiting, was this all that was in front of her? How could she be so stupid! Perhaps this was, in fact, what Q'ehazi had become. This idea was too horrific to contemplate, and Charli pushed it out of her mind, saying the word "No!" out loud and forcibly.

No matter, now that she was here, she was determined to learn what was ahead of her. Charli thought about retreating and attempting to go back to the creek, but that would mean giving up on her quest. Her curiosity was stronger than her fear, and it outweighed her trepidation about what she might experience in this world. She had to find out what this was and where this was. She reminded herself that the adventure of Q'ehazi only happened because she was brave enough to push forward, even though she didn't know what she would experience. Many people would turn back at this point, but not her. She was young and strong and brave.

While contemplating these thoughts to encourage herself to have faith in the future, Charli became aware that the lights she saw were coming from fires, many fires in the distance, that were also giving off that sulfur smell she'd noticed and contributing to the heat and dryness in the air. At least she could see a little more because the light from the distant fires was illuminating the area around her. She was walking across barren land that was vast and flat as far as she could see. The sounds of the screams and yells filled the air, and it was now impossible to deny that they were coming from people ahead who were probably trapped in the fires.

Charli moved on with ever decreasing speed, as the thought of wandering into that Hellscape was less and less appealing. Suddenly, she became aware that a person was barreling through the darkness toward her. She couldn't tell at this point if they were male or female, but they were running at great speed in her direction, as if they were running away from something terrifying. They were also screaming.

At this point, Charli stopped walking and waited—almost too terrified to breathe—as she saw that the person, whoever they were, was heading toward her at full speed.

Then, quite suddenly, the fleeing woman noticed Charli and her screams turned to entreaties. The words were in a language foreign to Charli, but she could understand the intensity of the woman's emotion and the state of her distress without needing any words to describe them. The woman's hair was matted and standing out from her head; her clothes were tattered and partially burned; her face was smeared with brown and black smudges; she was barefoot and appeared utterly exhausted. When she saw Charli, she stopped running and appeared to say something unintelligible, while shaking her head violently from side to side and bending over at the waist.

Charli wondered if she should offer assistance, so she moved closer to the woman and put out her hand in a gesture of support. The woman, however, seemed to misinterpret this and it only increased her fear. She started to run again and stumbled across the desolate landscape, obviously attempting to escape from something unimaginable, but to where Charli could not determine since there didn't seem to be anything in that direction to run toward, just more desolation and empty land.

At this point, Charli had no idea what to do, and her thought was to head back to where she'd come from since there didn't seem to be anything here to warrant her staying. Her own world was far from perfect, but it was certainly a lot better than this one. Her regret at having made the decision to come was a sharp pain in her side. *What had I been thinking?* This was definitely a bad idea. The best thing to do was to retrace her steps and hope to get back to her world before anything bad happened to her here.

As she was pondering her thoughts, Charli became aware now that more people were hurling themselves toward her and following the screaming woman. Charli could see that there were men and women, some were screaming and running away from their pursuers, and behind them were other people screaming but more from aggression than fear. Charli suddenly realized what the popping and crackling noises were. She remembered her mother's next-door neighbor who had a gun range outside his house where he shot squirrels and small birds for target practice; the sound was that of guns. Charli realized to her horror that some of the people screaming were being shot at and were falling down.

So, Charli ran. Stumbling blindly across the barren ground, she was grateful that there were no trees or any vegetation to impede her progress. She prayed that her steps would take her back to the place where she'd come from. Not wasting any of her breath to scream, her mind sharpened by panic, her mind repeating the same words over and over, *help me get back, please help me get back.* Charli had an innate sense of a God, or a Higher Power, or a Universe, that was in a position to protect her. That is what she prayed to now, knowing somehow intuitively, that this was not how it was supposed to end for her. She had made a mistake, certainly, but she was ultimately destined to return to Q'ehazi, and this was just a bad fork in the path from which she would and could recover.

Charli could still hear the screams and crackling behind her and still smell the acrid odor of sulfur in the air from the gunshots and fires. As her strong young legs carried her quickly across the ground, these things started to fade, and Charli thought she must be getting closer to the tear and the portal back to her own world, although she knew it could be difficult to recognize in this blackness.

Maybe she was lucky, or maybe there really was a God who was looking out for her. Up ahead, Charli became aware that the blue line that represented the junction between worlds was visible and still hovering in the air.

Charli stopped for a moment to catch her breath and glanced behind her. Through the gloom, she distinguished the shapes of people moving toward her, and so she knew she was still in significant danger. Yet again, she ran toward the blue line of the tear and got to it faster than she realized.

As soon as she stepped through the tear, she could feel the icy cold water of the creek beneath her feet, which was now a relief that she welcomed rather than disliked, almost as if the cold water jolted her back out of the nightmare and into reality that was far more comforting. Before leaving the creek, Charli had the presence of mind to close up the tear by pushing together the two halves as powerfully as she could, even while slipping on the icy rocks beneath her feet. Once she had managed to close up the tear, the blue line vanished, and Charli groped her way out of the creek, using her hands to balance her, until she was back on its rocky banks.

Charli sat on the ground for quite a while until her heartbeats regained their normal rhythm, her breathing slowed down, and the pressure in her chest eased. The trauma of the past few minutes was still vivid in her mind, and it would take time for her to come back to reality and fully realize that she was okay and safe. It was like being in a very realistic nightmarish dream, from which you awaken, and you have to remind yourself that it wasn't real, it was "just a dream".

Charli knew this wasn't just a dream, but an actual lived experience, although one that she could probably never fully explain to anyone in her world, any more than she could explain the Q'ehazi world. Charli kept looking in front of her, trying to see if the blue line of the tear was still there, and each time she failed to see it, reminding her that she had managed to escape successfully, and that nobody from that world could visit her world, for which she was extremely grateful.

Chapter Eight

As Barylos surveyed the barren landscape to which she and her followers had fled, she saw only beauty there. This land with its hard cold ground covered in snow, looked down upon by steely gray skies abundant with clouds, was beautiful because to her it represented freedom and power. Freedom from all the restrictions that had plagued her for her entire life; freedom to be who she chose without anyone judging her or hampering her; power to influence others in the way she thought best; and, most of all, freedom from her mother and all that she represented and from the Q'ehazi values that she had been born into but which to her were an anathema.

Barylos peered through the window of the stone building that housed her and her small band of devotees. The window glass was cracked and dirty, but it was still possible to make out the flat landscape stretching before her that was devoid of trees or other vegetation. Barylos was glad for the lack of trees or other evidence of nature around her. Even as a child, she had always hated nature and preferred to play alone or with her computer and concoct grand visions of what she saw as her future life as a leader with power and strength. Her mother was merely a woman who had been chosen as the sovereign of her people, based on her charm and charisma that Barylos interpreted as weakness and ineptitude. But Barylos was so much more than that. She had been raised as an ordinary citizen of the Q'ehazi, but she had always considered herself the daughter of a queen, and therefore worthy of special privileges, even if nobody else was cognizant of that.

Since Barylos was not deeply enamored of nature, she was happy to spend her time living in buildings rather than in the open air, as most of her Q'ehazi family favored. The peoples living far north of the Q'ehazi area had not managed to conquer the temperature and establish climate control, so Barylos and her followers were forced to be suffer the vagaries of the weather and its unpredictable shifts in temperature and moisture. Thus, all of her people lived in makeshift dwellings such as the one Barylos inhabited. Her future vision was an idea of huge glistening white cities full of tall and imposing structures (even carrying her name), as a demonstration of her enduring fame and power. Occasionally, she missed the regular three o'clock downpour with its wonderfully consistent level of rain to water the crops with the exact amount of water needed. But if and when she missed anything about normal Q'ehazi society, she would recapture for herself in her mind's eye one of those noble visions of her future life with all of its pomp and glamor.

Barylos breathed deeply, adjusted the belt on her khaki battle pants, and straightened her camouflage jacket. She was readying herself to give a presentation to her "Liberation Warriors" as she called them, and she wanted to look as presentable as she could. Her long dark hair was pulled back from her face in a severe bun, as she liked to give the impression that she was available to go into battle at any moment.

She could hear the noises of the other inhabitants of the building as they went about their business, also in preparation for the presentation from their leader. Those sounds were expected, and they comforted her, reassuring her that all was proceeding as it should. Just then she became aware of another sound that she hadn't expected, although it was not unpleasant to her ears: the din of a pack of yapping coyotes away in the distance. Gazing again through the window, she saw the dark forms of the wild dogs as they crossed the horizon. She wondered if this was some sort of sign or portent of good fortune. She reflected on how her "warriors" were also like a pack of wild dogs, operating together in close formation, able to take down what she saw as the failed and illegitimate society of the Q'ehazi world. That was her sole mission, as it always had been, when as a child she had felt misunderstood and undervalued.

Suddenly, the door behind her burst open and a young male soldier dressed in a uniform approached her breathlessly. He was tall and skinny, with a mop of black hair and long bangs hanging over his eyes on one side, that he constantly flicked away with one hand in a nervous gesture.

"Somebody here to see you, ma'am," he informed her, with a look and tone of urgency.

"I am *not* ma'am. I've told you before that I am Queen Barylos!" she snapped at the young man.

"Yes, yes, of course," the man fawned, bowing his head.

"Don't apologize. Just get it right next time. Who is here to see me?"

"It's Manteen back from his mission to visit Aurora, your mother, Queen Barylos."

"Fine, let him approach."

The man left the room and was replaced in a few moments by an older man, with gray hair and a wizened face. His uniform was tattered, and his face was lined with worry and dirt.

"Manteen, it's good to see you." Even though there were a couple of chairs in the room and the man panted with exhaustion, Barylos did not offer to let him sit down. "What information have you discovered for me?" she demanded.

The man's voice was raspy and cracked, whether from age or fatigue it was hard to tell.

"I infiltrated the Q'ehazi successfully, as you required," he responded, drawing himself up into a readied posture.

"My injury proved to be a sufficient excuse, and I visited Joslyn in his surgery for treatment for the wound. Due to the injury, I couldn't travel very fast so it was a hard journey to get there."

"I don't want to hear about the journey. Tell me the outcome." Barylos fixed him with a steely glare, making no effort to contain her impatience. "I want to know what you found out."

"Yes, Queen. I managed to speak to Aurora."

"So, you spoke to her? Did she know who you were?"

"She knows I hailed originally from the Q'ehazi Village of Mechanics Southwest. I waited until I was rested enough to walk normally before visiting her, and I didn't reveal that I had been treated by her son."

"Very good. Go on."

"I pretended to be concerned for her safety and that of the Q'ehazi people. I asked her if she had any weapons she could use if they were attacked."

A slow smile started to spread across Barylos' face as she heard this, and she nodded as if agreeing with the question. "What did she say to that?"

"She seemed surprised that I would ask that. She replied, as I thought she would, that they don't have weapons. They will respond to any attack in the way they always have. That's what she said. The Q'ehazi principles of peace and understanding will not be relinquished, even under duress. Those were her exact words, Queen."

Barylos' smile broadened. "Perfect. That is also what I expected her to say. Because she has no idea what damage weapons can do when they are in the right hands—MY hands and the hands of my people, my warriors." Her pride was evident in her voice. "It is as I thought. They are completely unprepared for what is going to happen to them. I am glad. It is what they deserve."

"Exactly," agreed the man, although his voice lacked the conviction Barylos wished to hear, either through his extreme fatigue or through an element of inner resistance to her words, she couldn't tell.

"Go and rest," she ordered. "You have done well," she placated the man, realizing his usefulness and wishing him to conserve his energy for future campaigns.

The man bowed briefly and left the room. The younger man returned and saluted Barylos, then stood at attention awaiting more orders.

Barylos spent a couple of moments in thought before addressing her young soldier. "We need to be sure we perfect the making of the guns," she mused aloud. "How is that progressing?"

"It's going well," enthused the young man. "We now have 50 guns, all ready."

"Fifty? That's not nearly enough. How many of us are there now?"

"Almost a hundred," the man responded eagerly, "and growing every day."

"We will not be ready to attack until the majority of us have a firearm that is loaded and ready to use."

The man's face appeared crest-fallen by this information. "That will take a long time."

"Then you need to speed up the process. We don't have time to waste. Get it done!" commanded Barylos.

"But I," stammered the young man, unsure how to respond.

"Do you want to be the one responsible for the failure of our mission?" barked Barylos.

"No, ma'am, I mean, uh, Queen, of course."

"Then do whatever it takes!"

Chapter Nine

The next thing Charli realized was that the *Pukatl* fruit she had brought with her to access the portal to Q'ehazi was exactly where she had placed it moments before discovering the ruby stone. It was in the pocket of her jacket that was on the ground beside the Redbud Tree. A wave of relief washed over her at the knowledge that this precious item was still there. She wondered, in fact, if she had "lost time" while being in the other world. But when she checked her watch, she saw that she had spent about a half an hour undergoing that experience, and it was now 3:30 in the afternoon.

Charli rested for a moment on the ground, breathing deeply the scent of the pure, clean air, feeling supremely grateful now for her own world, with all its problems, as it was certainly far superior to the world she had just left.

When she had collected herself sufficiently, she rose deliberately to her feet. This time she knew what to do because the memory of her process for entering the portal had now entered her consciousness like a leaf ascending to the surface of a still pond. She now remembered very clearly the ritual she had employed many years before when going through the portal and into the Q'ehazi world. There was still some trepidation, as she wondered if she really could enter that world again or if it had changed a lot since her last visit. But she pushed down her hesitancy, retrieved and held up the fruit, while placing her hand on the bark of the tree. Almost at once, the familiar brown line appeared in the air and hovered there tantalizingly.

The appearance of the line provoked less excitement in Charli that it might have done if she hadn't just undergone the nightmarish experience of the Hellscape World. She had confidence that the ruby stone had been buried beneath the tree for a reason, and its purpose there was designed specifically so that she, Charli, could return to the erstwhile home she had known for just a brief period five years earlier. Her loss of the ruby stone didn't faze her, as the *Pukatl* fruit was probably enough to allow access back into Q'ehazi.

She did, however, feel a sense of a cycle finally completed, a sense that her time had come, and she was fated to step through the portal again and into the Q'ehazi world, come what may.

Charli had been through many trials and tribulations over the past five years since her last visit to Q'ehazi. These included the turbulent relationship with Nick; her change of direction in a career choice; coming to terms with the loss of her beloved grandfather, which had provoked unexpected closeness with her mother and the burgeoning of their relationship as equals; and the unrest and disillusionment she saw all around in her own world, where it seemed that rampant corruption and greed always outweighed care for the planet or empathy for others. Through all these challenges, Charli had been fixated on this one idea that a world existed where good triumphed, where love prevailed, and grace was valued. She had found and lost that world once before. This time, if she was really given a second chance, she would make the best use of it.

Charli had been a girl when she first discovered Q'ehazi, a mere 16-year-old, with innate wisdom for sure, but without much direct experience of the world. Now, she was a woman who had seen and experienced more. She knew who she was and what she valued and wanted in life. What she desired more than anything else was to be a part of that domain where she felt she belonged, so much more than the one she'd been born into.

So, with a heavy sigh and a mixture of finality and determination, Charli pulled the tear apart until she had created a hole large enough to step through, and she stepped through the opening and into the other universe.

As she had experienced before, all those years ago, even though at first glance the world seemed exactly the same to her sight, the air seemed sweeter here, the sounds more musical, and the colors more intense and vivid. Her spirits were buoyant, as she strode across the grass, taking a familiar direction toward what she knew was the village where her friends Abbe and Sovereign Aurora and Joslyn lived. Charli felt an intense mixture of emotions inside her: excitement that bubbled up in her stomach, an ache in her chest that felt like longing for the life she'd wanted for so long, and a flutter of nervousness at the thought that perhaps things had changed or that people wouldn't remember her after all. But she made certain her steps were confident and strong, and with every stride closer to the Village of Musicians where Abbe lived, she felt more and more certain she had done the right thing by coming here.

Away in the distance, she could hear some noises that created a peaceful harmony with the songs of birdcalls and industrious cicadas around her. Other sounds included the high floating notes of something like a flute; a human voice singing, but too distant to be able to distinguish words or a definite tune; and the rhythmic beating of drums. These sounds reassured her that the Q'ehazi world she had known was still that vibrant, musical place she had experienced before, and her steps became faster and faster as she pushed ahead.

She could see on the horizon that there was a gathering of people in the distance, which possibly included the musicians and singers she could hear, along with an audience of some size. Charli felt the smile on her face broaden, as she anticipated the welcome she would receive.

As she came closer, she saw a group of about 20 men and women of all ages and colors seated on the ground in a circular formation around the four musicians playing some kind of wind instrument, a percussion instrument, and a stringed instrument that resembled a cross between a guitar and a violin. The assembly all had smiles on their faces, showing that they were thoroughly enjoying the concert being performed for them. The musicians were too engrossed in their performance to really notice as Charli approached.

The music was joyful and vivacious, and Charli was pleased by the happiness she saw on the faces of the spectators. As she got close enough to make eye contact with one of the audience members, they smiled at her and made a space for her so she could join in and watch the performance.

The familiar thought-words from the woman beside her were, "Welcome. Come and join us." Charli sat on the grass and a flood of memories assailed her from an earlier time, a time when she had sat on this same grass and listened, but that time it was a religious or spiritual ceremony. In that instance, she had been sitting next to a very important person: Joslyn, who had inspired in her feelings she had never experienced before as a 16-year-old girl with limited experience of the other sex, due to being home-schooled during the start of the pandemic and relatively isolated.

The nostalgia for that moment, with its mix of unexpected emotions, created an ache in her chest that was in contrast to the joy of the moment. But Charli welcomed all of these feelings. She felt as though the life she had at "home" in her "real" world was but a pale shadow of this one. She had been sleep-walking through that life, doing what was expected of her and making decisions and choices that seemed sensible, but not really living fully, as she did here in Q'ehazi.

Charli contemplated these things as the piece of music finished, and the audience expressed their appreciation in the traditional Q'ehazi way, swaying and holding hands and sending their silent appreciation to the performers.

It was only then that Charli recognized the girl playing the stringed instrument. *Could it be her?* Yes, it was her friend Abbe, the sweet and enthusiastic girl she had known five years before, who still looked almost exactly the same, with the same radiant smile, the same lithe athletic body, and the same wild black hair that framed her oval dark-skinned face.

Charli was so thrilled to see her friend that she stood up and waved to her excitedly.

When Abbe recognized Charli, her excitement matched that of the other girl's joy, and they ran toward each other and gave each other the longest and most affectionate hug imaginable. Charli savored the sweetness of her friend's gesture with a relief she hadn't anticipated.

"You came. You're here., I can't quite believe it!" Abbe's thought-words cascaded into Charli's head, and she matched them: "I wanted to come back for so long. I'm so happy to be here."

Finally, the two girls pulled away from the hug and gazed at each other's eyes, with expressions of wonder and happiness.

"You found the stone?"

"Yes, of course. Did you bury it?"

"Yes. I knew you'd come. I told mother you'd come and help us. I *knew* you'd come back."

It took a couple of minutes for Charli's mind to accommodate her friend's last sentence. "What do you mean, help you? Why do you need help?"

Abbe gave a long sigh that seemed to have an even longer story behind it. "Perhaps my mother should explain. Do you want to join us for dinner?"

"Well, of course. I don't have anything better to do!" The two girls giggled, as they had done that first day they'd met when they were both teenagers.

Abbe took Charli's hand. "Give me a minute to collect my things and then we'll walk over. Mother and Joslyn are dining with the Village of the Architects tonight, and I promised to join them. I'm sure they won't mind if you're there, too!"

At the mention of Joslyn's name, Charli's heart skipped a beat, and she hoped her friend didn't notice the expression on her face subtly alter. "That would be great, thank you," she responded with her thought-words.

The journey over to the other village was a long walk of roughly a mile and a half. Charli was glad she'd remembered to wear her sneakers that were relatively comfortable for walking. She was also grateful that the weather was the typical 73° and dry that was always maintained in Q'ehazi at this time of day, so her light jacket was plenty for her, even as the cooler evening air started to descend on them.

As they ambled across the ground through a forested area and between fields and meadows peppered with crops and vegetation, the two girls conversed in thought-language and caught up with each other's lives. Abbe was most curious to find out about what Charli was doing in her world, so Charli recounted to her friend all about her studies at college, graduating with her Master's, moving to Raleigh, and setting a goal to become a psychologist. Charli left out all mention of the unsatisfying relationship she'd had with Nick and the mistakes she felt she'd made in the romance department.

Charli was equally curious to find out all about her companion's adventures and goals. Abbe described how her musical career was flourishing, and she'd become involved with a "wonderful man" who was everything she wanted in a relationship. Charli looked away and tried to act casual as she inquired about Joslyn. "I suppose he's married by now, is he?"

"No, he was with a girl for a while, somebody he met through his work, but that didn't last. I asked Mother if I should introduce him to some of my female friends, but she says, 'Allow him to make his own choices.' You know how she is!"

Charli couldn't help a small flutter of happiness at Abbe's remarks, and she squeezed her friend's hand a little tighter, as they continued to meander across the grass and toward the place where Abbe's family was expecting her.

When they arrived, Charli did not at first recognize the tall black man with the warm brown eyes and full beard. But when he approached her with arms outstretched and a broad smile, she felt all at once as if her whole body was glowing.

"Joslyn!" she couldn't help exclaiming aloud, as he gave her a hug that enveloped her in arms that were strong yet tender. She remembered the sweet musky scent of him. She could feel her heart beating in her chest so powerfully that she wondered if he could feel it, too, if he could sense the impact he still had on her. When he drew away and looked at her, his gaze was appreciative.

"You've become a woman, Charli. Last time I saw you, you were still a little girl." There was no need for speech from him, his thought-words were communicated clearly, and Charli responded, "That's right. And you, too." She could see that the boy she had met five years ago had now become a man, his build more powerful and complete, with the beard giving him an impression of maturity he had not possessed before.

"Are you still working as a healer?" Charli was genuinely interested to know.

"Yes, of course. I have expanded my practice and help people from several nearby villages now. And you?"

Charli considered for a moment. "Yes, I am a healer too, but of the mind." Joslyn appeared confused by her statement, so she explained. "In my world, the mind and body are separate, not like in yours."

"So many things are different. But come, my mother will be so pleased to see you again." With that, Joslyn ushered Charli over to the long dining table set with plates and silverware, and guided her to sit at a spot between himself and his sister Abbe and across the table from their mother, Sovereign Aurora.

As Charli was walking over to the main table, she noticed all of the people entering this secluded grassy area. Many were smiling and laughing as if they knew each other and were communicating telepathically, and all of them were carrying dishes containing food of various kinds. Some of them brought raw vegetables perhaps plucked from their own gardens; some cooked meals; and some provided other foodstuffs such as fish, bread, and chicken. Each dish was handed to the man and woman standing at the head of a long table where the dishes were being laid, and everything was gratefully accepted. Charli wondered if this kind of a "potluck" meal was a regular occurrence or due to some festive event taking place. Her inner question was answered by Joslyn, as he saw her noticing the arriving guests with their contributions, and he responded to her in thought-words. "Everything is done on a barter system here, so people all bring a contribution to the feast in order to attend."

"Oh, I see, rather than money, you mean?" Charli had blurted her question before remembering that the Q'ehazi did not use money in their society. Upon noticing Joslyn's confused expression, she blushed, "Sorry, I forgot." But there was no more time for embarrassment because Charli had now arrived at the table where Sovereign Aurora and the rest of her family had their seats, and Joslyn motioned for her to be seated.

Charli could see Sovereign Aurora talking to a little group of people a few feet away, who were obviously needing her guidance on something. After a few moments, Aurora returned to the table, and when she saw Charli, her face broke out into a beaming smile, and she gave Charli the customary hug. "My dear, it is so good to see you!"

Charli noticed that the older woman had a few more lines on her face and her hair was beginning to turn gray at the temples, but she still moved with the lithe agility of someone much younger, and her body was slim and strong. Not as tall as her son, she still was taller than average and had a demeanor that had an air of authority without being imposing or harsh. Charli thought she detected a different expression in Aurora's eyes than she'd seen before, a hint of sadness or melancholy that hadn't been there before.

Charli was introduced to Serano, Abbe and Joslyn's father, and although at first his somber outlook was a little disconcerting to her, in time she got used to his dour countenance and began to enjoy his occasional interjections into the conversations and his quiet wisdom.

After the customary holding hands and saying of thanks to the Great Creator for the food they would consume, people mostly ate in silence. Charli remembered from her previous visit how the Q'ehazi custom was to give full attention to the eating of food without distractions of small talk. Thought-words were used for individual comments on practical subjects, and the sharing of more important information was carried out as they sat around the firepit later that evening and spoke aloud.

It wasn't until that point that Charli learned what had been happening in Q'ehazi since her departure five years earlier. Due to some of the comments made by other people in the group, Charli picked up that the circumstances of the Q'ehazi people had not all been good. When Serano mentioned *The Great Sickness* that had ravaged all of their society, Charli asked for more information and was horrified to discover that it sounded as if COVID 19 had not left these people unscathed.

"It was Maudina who first told us of her dream about the virus and *The Great Sickness*," the Sovereign admitted, "and quite quickly afterwards, unfortunately, her dream came true."

"I always knew she was a prophet," a man chimed in.

"So sad that *The Great Sickness* claimed Maudina as one of the first victims," spoke a woman.

"Oh no!" gasped Charli as she put her hand to her mouth. "You don't mean?"

"Yes, my dear, Maudina died about four years ago. We still miss her terribly."

Charli felt her eyes fill with tears. She hadn't realized how much she loved the Sovereign's sister, the woman who helped her take Sean back to the portal and who seemed so full of life and vitality the last time she saw her.

"I remember her telling me about the dream. I thought it was just that I had told her about our world and the virus killing all the people." Charli suddenly had a horrible revelation. "I found out later that Sean had the virus. So, was it Sean who brought the virus into Q'ehazi? Oh my God!" This shocking thought knocked Charli back on her seat and froze her in that position.

Aurora regarded her sympathetically, "My dear, there is no need for guilt or remorse. What happened, happened and we survived ultimately and that's the main thing."

Charli felt her eyes filling with tears again, but this time they were tears that stung her as they fell because they were tears of sadness and rage. "He brought the virus to you. How could he? How could he?" She knew her words were just an outpouring of emotion and that the question was rhetorical. She also knew that most of her anger was directed towards herself for being so stupid as to let that happen to her beloved Q'ehazi world.

Sovereign Aurora gently stroked her shoulders, and the others murmured comforting words. The rest of the conversation fell silent for a few moments, as everybody felt the intensity of Charli's pain.

Joslyn spoke next, saying, "We found to our dismay that the *Pukatl* herb was no use against *The Great Sickness*. At first, many people died, and we were heart-broken. But we had to carry on, and so we started confining the sickest of our people in our buildings."

"Something, as you know, we had never done before," Abbe contributed.

"We were forced to keep them apart from the healthy people because we knew that *The Great Sickness* was very easily transmitted.

The healthy people also wore face coverings, and for a while we stopped our usual custom of hugging strangers and friends."

"Isolation and masks," Charli repeated, glumly. These things were horribly familiar to her.

"Our scientists and doctors set about researching a cure. After a few months, they started healing people, at least the ones who were the least infected."

"Meanwhile, we put a lot of emphasis on prevention," Aurora offered, "because we knew that with a very healthy strong immune system, it was less likely that the disease would take hold."

Joslyn continued, "Gradually, over months and months, there were fewer and fewer cases. We started to come out of our buildings, and even started to hug again and to remove the face coverings. But the experience changed us, made us less trusting maybe, and less open to strangers."

"I am so sad," Charli couldn't help admitting.

"I know, my dear," the Sovereign reassured her. "The Q'ehazi people are not perfect, but we are still strong and resilient, and we will bounce back fully. Everything that happens teaches us something valuable, and we are wiser and stronger for it. Yes, even the painful things."

"It shouldn't have happened to you," said Charli, feeling her anger rise again.

"There are no 'shoulds' in this world," Aurora reassured her, "only tests and mistakes and lessons learned."

Abbe spoke now and seemed to be very keen to impart information to her friend. The girlish enthusiasm she had once possessed was replaced by a passion that was as intense and had an edge to it born of the fire she had been through: "We are over *The Great Sickness*. Nobody has died or become ill from it for a long time. But we are facing something much worse. Another kind of sickness, which is a sickness of the spirit not the body."

"What do you mean?" asked Charli, genuinely mystified.

"She is talking about Barylos," responded Joslyn, in a resigned tone.

"Do you remember Barylos?" asked Aurora.

"Yes, I do. She was your other daughter," said Charli. "I remember she didn't like me much."

Abbe gave a little ironic chuckle.

"She has become quite powerful now," said Serano, who had spoken earlier and introduced the topic of *The Great Sickness*.

"Powerful?"

"She thinks *she* should be sovereign, or *Queen* as she calls it," agreed another woman.

"But why on earth would she think this?" Charli was so amazed by hearing this information that she couldn't fathom what was going on. This truly *was* worse than the virus infecting the people physically, from which they seemed to have recovered.

"As you know, we Q'ehazi don't choose our leaders based on their lineage or their genetic history, but based on their ability to achieve a *State of Grace*, their wisdom, and their ability to help and guide others. But in Barylos' mind, the fact that she is my daughter, and my older daughter, gives her the automatic right to inherit the mantle of leader from me."

Aurora sighed deeply and took a long drink from her glass of water before continuing. The others were silent, recognizing that what needed to be explained was better coming from their Sovereign than anybody else.

"Barylos rejects the Q'ehazi values and customs. She always did, but her ideas became much more crystallized within her following *The Great Sickness* and its effects on our people. She stopped using the *Pukatl* herb, which she said destroyed her strength and power. She disagreed with our efforts to keep people safe and healthy and started spreading lies about how we were killing people by locking them up in buildings and withholding medication. She started to garner support among those who felt lost or disaffected, and she gradually amassed what she calls an 'Army of Liberation Warriors' who, she says she will use to overcome our society by force someday."

"I feel this is partly my responsibility. I raised her as a child, and I should have seen the seeds of this within her and made an effort to stop her. It is true that the sickness she displays is far more virulent than the physical sickness we lived through, and it is much more difficult to contain or eradicate. I had to excommunicate her from our land. My own daughter! But it was necessary to do this, as she was proving potentially dangerous to my people. I don't even know exactly where she is, but it's somewhere far to the north of here." As Aurora said these words, her body seemed to be pulled down by the weight of the terrible burden she felt, and she appeared exhausted by the effort of even talking about it.

"This is where *you* come in," explained Abbe, taking up the mantle from her mother. "I had a feeling you could help us, and so I suggested burying the ruby stone beneath the Redbud Tree so that you could visit us again."

Charli felt a wave of relief and recognition wash over her. "Oh, I see!" she expostulated. "I'm sure I can help you. I will find a way. After all, I'm the one who brought the person here who had the virus."

"You didn't exactly *bring* him," Abbe remarked.

"Yes, I know. I didn't know he followed me here, but I'm still indirectly responsible. So, it makes sense that I should be the person to help you." Charli felt almost gratified she finally had the opportunity to make a difference here in her beloved Q'ehazi. They needed her, and she was potentially the only person who could help them.

"How will you help us?" asked Serano. Night had fallen and the light was faint from the firepit they were seated around. Because they were in a group setting, people were speaking aloud, and Charli recognized the low tones of her friend's father resonating through the gloom.

Charli looked around her at the expectant faces of the 20 or so people who were seated on the ground. They were all studying her intently and waiting for her to say something significant that would impact their lives and pull them out of their current predicament. For the first time in her young life, Charli had the experience of feeling really needed and important. This was something she had always longed for, and yet the responsibility of it was scary and heavy. She had to respond honestly and with integrity, while inspiring them with confidence that she could do something that would make a difference.

"I don't know yet," she admitted, "but I am going to use Maudina's dream incubation techniques tonight as I aim to discover an answer that will help you by tomorrow morning." There was a palpable sense of relief among the people after her stated intention, and Charli knew she would have to put her words into action and offer something concrete. She didn't know how she was going to accomplish the goal she had set herself, but she believed she could find a way.

With all of the intense emotions Charli had experienced that day, by the time the post-dinner musical interludes were completed and everybody was getting ready for bed, she felt so drained she could hardly keep her eyes open. She dragged herself up the small wooden steps that led to her hammock in the trees and made herself comfortable with the down-filled coverlet and pillows that had been provided for her. Small flickering lights from nearby candles were visible amid the gathering gloom of nightfall, and Charli enjoyed listening to the hum of night sounds around her from insects, night birds, and small creatures that awakened at dusk and carried out their activities while the humans were still asleep.

Charli remembered the instructions Maudina had given about dream incubation and tried to recall them more clearly, as it had been five years since she had spent time with the Director of the Dreams Academy in Q'ehazi. From her recollection, it was important to meditate upon the question you wished answered or the guidance you wished to receive in your dreams. Charli attempted to hold this idea—*How can I help the Q'ehazi with their current problems?*—in her mind long enough to meditate upon it, but in only a few moments drowsiness overcame her completely and she was unable to resist the urge to sleep.

Chapter Ten

Charli slept well that night in her hammock next to Abbe, and she experienced vivid and strange dreams, although they were confusing and difficult to interpret.

As soon as dawn pricked the corners of her eyes with its soft light, she awoke and went strolling in the woods to meditate and attempt to collect her thoughts, tasked as she was to come up with an answer that would help these people and absolve her for the mistakes that had caused her to bring these challenges into their world.

Following Aurora's recommendations, Charli "put the big stick down" that she'd been beating herself up with, realizing that it did no good to castigate herself for the unfortunate circumstances for which she was partly responsible. The only thing that mattered was how she could help find a solution to the current situation in Q'ehazi that would change things in a positive way.

Her dreams had been scattered and puzzling, but Charli believed she could assemble the clues from the piecemeal bits of information, images, and thoughts she woke up with that morning, following her dream incubation question.

In one dream fragment, Charli was submerged in water and called out to Joslyn to help save her, but she was unable to find him. In a second fragment, she saw Barylos before her, who suddenly became an animal—a hyena with snarling fangs. In a third fragment, Charli saw herself as Queen Boadicea (the Celtic queen who led a revolt against Roman rule in ancient times) riding into battle on a horse with her long flowing hair cascading behind her. Charli tried to piece together all of these fragments into a meaningful whole that would guide her in how to act at this important juncture.

Was she really a savior for these people or was that her ego talking? Was she a young woman who lacked purpose in her "real" world and so sought it in this place? All of the old doubts about herself and her worth crowded into her mind and distracted her from her mission. She thrust away these thoughts, rejecting them like an unwanted lover, knowing how useless they were. "Nothing matters except helping these people," she reminded herself. "They asked me to come here. I have some resources from my world that I can use to help them. The Q'ehazi have never experienced these things before, so they are like innocents who trust in others and don't understand greed or envy or hate. I have encountered all of those things and developed defenses against them, and I know of resources within and without me to aid and guide them."

Charli picked up a beautiful multi-colored leaf and focused her mind on it, clearing her mind of anything else that was distracting or self-sabotaging.

Charli attempted to see inside Barylos' mind, to ascertain the woman's true goals. Barylos had always been jealous of the "stranger" from another world. Barylos hated the way her mother paid more attention to Charli than to her own eldest daughter. Barylos still had not attained the wished-for *State of Grace* that was every Q'ehazi's goal. She had already spurned the notion of a *State of Grace* altogether and had headed in another direction, one that Charli knew well.

Charli had come across people like that in her own world, some she knew personally and others were celebrities she'd only read about. These were people who lusted after money and the power that money brought them; people who considered themselves superior to others as a birthright; and people who did not consider all men and women equal, but rather wished to exert their authority over others for their own exclusive benefit.

Charli had encountered in her former boyfriend Nick, a man who tried to control her and exert his influence and authority over her, who tried to deny her independence, and who twisted her version of reality to fit his narrative where he was the protector and not the perpetrator of the violence and betrayal manifested in their relationship. Charli thought about how that was reflected on a grander scale by some of the politicians, media moguls, and powerful wealthy people in her world.

Then a thought came to her that made her smile a little. An individual like Barylos didn't fit in with the Q'ehazi society of tolerance and equality, but maybe she would be well-suited to her *own world* where money and power were more important than anything else. In the same way as Charli felt she was more accepted in Q'ehazi than she was in her own world, the reverse could equally be said to be true that Barylos was a better match for Charli's world where money trumped everything else.

Another fragment of a dream came back to Charli, and all of a sudden it fit in her mind like the last piece of a jigsaw puzzle. The face of Barylos was that of a hyena, a face vindictive and self-serving, cunning, and sly with a ruthless ambition that could not be quelled. Charli was also an animal, but one that seemed less threatening on the outside. She was a deer, gentle and peace-loving, munching on grass. When she saw the tiny red eyes of the hyena, she felt fear, but she also felt a strange sense of power. She ran from the predator, knowing that it would follow her. She ran and ran for a long time, knowing what was up ahead, and plotted the outcome of this chase.

At the last second, she turned away from the jagged edges of a steep cliff just in time to rescue herself. From the top of the cliff, she saw the hyena careening off the edge of the cliff and plunging to its death on the rocks below, having been tricked into chasing what it thought was its prey and eventually killing itself instead.

Charli knew now what she would do and what she would tell the people. She would entice Barylos into her world and coerce her into leaving Q'ehazi for good, along with all her followers, thus ridding the Q'ehazi people of their scourge.

Her next thought filled Charli with an odd sort of glee, as well as a guilty pang at the idea. Barylos and her followers knew nothing of that horrific and terrifying world Charli had unexpectedly and unwillingly encountered. Could she trick them into entering that world and remaining there unable to escape? Charli even chuckled aloud at the wayward idea that Barylos and Sean might meet up in the dark and dangerous world where they both deserved to be.

In either case, it would mean finding a way to infiltrate the Barylos stronghold and communicating with her directly, persuading her somehow to leave Q'ehazi for what she would perceive as a better opportunity for both her and her army of followers. The main thing was to rid the Q'ehazi world of this infection once and for all by cutting it off at the source and destroying the cancerous tumor forever.

With a renewed sense of purpose and determination, Charli strode over to the village where she met Aurora and the others the evening before. She spotted the Sovereign in a clearing seated on a tree trunk chair with her long white gown flowing from under her feet. A middle-aged woman knelt before the Sovereign with her face contorted in distress or pain. Aurora placed her hands gently on the woman's shoulders with her eyes closed. She helped the woman in some way because, after a few moments, the woman's body relaxed and she stood up re-invigorated.

Since a few people were waiting in a haphazard line for the Sovereign's guidance or help, Charli wasn't sure if she was allowed or expected to break in line with her request. To her relief, Aurora turned to her and waved for her to come forward before the next supplicant. Instead of using thought-words, Charli whispered to Aurora that she was ready to help the Q'ehazi people with her new solution. Aurora thanked Charli in thought-words and encouraged her to enjoy breakfast before the official meeting.

After the majority of people in the village finished their breakfast, Sovereign Aurora asked the town crier to make a holler announcement so that people from neighboring villages could gather around to hear Charli's special message for them. The formal meeting would convene later that day in the early evening before dinner. While waiting for that event, Charli felt a nervous apprehension. She wondered if she could explain her intentions in such a way that people would understand and agree with her ideas. This was the first time any authority had been given to her, and she was unsure whether she was up for the challenge.

Charli felt infused with a strength and wisdom she'd never realized before. Perhaps it was because she was in Q'ehazi that she felt different, or perhaps it was because, for the first time, she was suddenly called to draw from the well of her experiences and plumb the depths of her talent in finding an answer that was incredibly important.

"You two are liars and thieves!"

Hearing raised voices in Q'ehazi was so unusual that Charli was taken aback at seeing the young white male yelling at his brown female counterpart, while pointing an accusatory finger. The girl receiving this onslaught, backed away, and placed a trembling hand on her husband's shoulder. "We are not what you say," pleaded her spouse. "You refused to listen to our explanations."

The young man let out an expletive and flung his hands up in disgust. "Why should I listen to you when all you say is a lie?" He turned to the watching crowd seated around the arguing threesome in an observant circle. "These people, my neighbors, Tali and Bundo, didn't give me what they owed me, what they had agreed to give me."

"We *did* give you that," exclaimed Tali in plaintive tones. "We gave you the chickens as agreed. What more do you want?"

"Oh, yes, *now* you give them, but only after I repeatedly asked and reminded you," came the rejoinder from Bartok, the young man, who had now gone red in the face from all his yelling.

"As Tali told you before, we were both away for several months tending to my sick mother in a village on the other side of the mountain. When we got back, we had forgotten all about our debt to you. But we apologized and tried to make it up to you. We don't appreciate all of your insults." Bundo was tall and thin with coffee-colored skin and short dark-red hair. He had a deep resonant voice that inspired confidence in those who listened. The crowd was watchful, but nobody interjected. They were an audience of villagers observing the exchange between neighbors with a detached interest.

Now Bundo turned to the onlookers and addressed them. "Bartok is correct that we did not give him the chickens right away, but he is only telling you half of the story. He could have asked us earlier, and we would gladly have recompensed him."

Bartok sneered to suggest his disbelief at Bundo's comment.

At this point, another person joined the fray in the center of the ensemble. Sovereign Aurora had been hovering in the background and observing alongside the crowd. She took center stage and spoke aloud in her deep, melodious voice that inspired both calm and respect. "We have heard your respective arguments. We see that you all are angry. Yet, as many of us realize, underneath anger there is often fear. So, I am going to ask you each a question. First you, Bartok, what is it that you fear?"

The young man was momentarily taken aback by her question. He briefly stepped out of the cloud of his anger to see the situation from a different perspective. The red color drained from his face and was replaced by a normal pinkish hue. He spoke in subdued tones as he replied, "I don't believe I'm afraid of anything."

Aurora didn't reply but stood looking at him without speaking, as if to say, "I'm going to wait here for your actual answer."

Bartok weighed the pros and cons. His mask of defiance dropped, and his manner was authentic and vulnerable as he replied, "My wife and I needed those chickens. Our whole brood was killed by a fox a few nights ago. It didn't matter at first, and I just let it go, but today it matters a great deal."

"Were you afraid that Bundo and Tali might never give you the chickens they owed you?"

"I was afraid that my wife and I would starve."

"Did your neighbors know about this misfortune that had befallen you?"

"I didn't tell them that as I didn't think it was their business."

"Yet all of your anger and emotions were related to the unfortunate incident that occurred. Maybe they had a right to know what was fueling your anger. Perhaps they would have understood your challenging situation and acted sooner."

Bartok and the others were silent, and the young man nodded in recognition of Aurora's conclusion.

She turned promptly to the other two who had been confronted by Bartok. "And you, Tali and Bundo, why are you so angry with your neighbor?"

Tali was a pretty, dark-haired girl who looked younger than her husband. "We were angry with Bartok for insulting us and calling us names. We didn't deserve that. We never stole anything from him."

"I will ask you the same question. What is the fear underneath the anger?"

Bundo was the first to respond. "We have to preserve our good reputation. Especially for Tali, as she is a healer, and her patients respect her. Being maligned in this way could hurt us, especially if Bartok attempts some reprisal for our supposed misdeeds."

"I would never do that," blurted Bartok.

"We don't know that," exclaimed Tali, her voice again raised in exasperation.

Aurora raised her arms in a calming gesture, and everybody dropped their aggressive stance.

"There is assumption and misunderstanding on both sides. Can you all agree to let this go and be friends again? Bartok lost his chickens and was fearful for his family's security; Bundo was worried about his sick mother; and Tali was nervous that her reputation had been damaged. Yet at this moment, you are all fine and well."

Charli thought she heard a murmuring from the crowd and, at the same time, it wasn't something she heard exactly, but a group-thought, that was being passed through the air like a spontaneous wave of positive enthusiasm. "All fine and well, all fine and well, all fine and well...." She looked around and saw that everyone in the group of watchers was swaying in a sort of rhythm, with smiles on their faces, as if willing the combatants to join them in their dance of peace and harmony. When these three finally caught the wave and embraced each other in a moment of genuine reconciliation, the crowd let out a collective sigh of pleasure and relief. Then Charli joined in.

Charli realized that she had seen another *Fairness Test* that was a hallmark of the Q'ehazi way of settling disputes. She reflected on how this might have been handled back home in her world. Perhaps a legal battle would focus on the law's interpretation of events without any relation to the context involved for all the participants. Perhaps the hostilities would have escalated to the point where actual physical harm was inflicted on one or more of the disputing neighbors. It would have been unlikely that the people involved would reach a greater understanding of each other's predicament as had happened here.

Charli was also struck by the way the onlookers did not automatically take sides. They allowed all of the people to speak and tell their truth from their point of view, so that equal weight was given to both sides of the argument and nobody was immediately deemed right or wrong.

What a difference, in every way, from her own world! Charli reflected again on the irony of the situation. She was so much more aligned with the Q'ehazi values that had been demonstrated here, while Barylos, the daughter of the Q'ehazi sovereign, was more attuned to the values of Charli's own world.

Later that day, addressing an assembly of about 100 people and following Sovereign Aurora's introduction of her to the crowd, Charli outlined her plan. "I will journey to visit Barylos," she announced. "I will tell her about *my* world, which is another universe parallel to this one but very different. In my world, she can be rich and powerful because all she needs to do is take some of the ruby stones with her from Q'ehazi and sell them, which is what Sean was intending to do, although he got sick and never fulfilled that intention. I will make sure she takes all of her followers with her and that she leaves Q'ehazi forever and never returns." Charli did not, at this stage, mention her plan to take Barylos and her followers into the Hellscape World instead, partly because she wasn't sure if that goal was even attainable, and partly because she felt that the main point to get across was Barylos' exclusion from the Q'ehazi world, which was the most important thing now.

Some of the people watching and listening murmured their agreement or approval.

"This sounds very dangerous, young Charli," said Aurora, with a concerned expression. "What if Barylos wishes harm to you?"

"She probably *does* wish harm to me, but she will realize that I am the only one who can lead her and her followers to the other world where she will benefit, and so it is in her own self-interest to keep me alive so that she can fulfill her goals."

"It is true that Barylos wishes only for power, and this is a way to let her have it," agreed Abbe. "Are you sure she will be accepted into your world?"

"Once she has amassed a lot of money, she will certainly be accepted," answered Charli. "Money is everything in my world, as it is nothing in yours."

"What about the toxic air?" mentioned Joslyn. "I understand that the air in your world makes a Q'ehazi person very sick."

"Many people in my world are still wearing face masks because they are afraid of COVID-19. She could prevent the air from hitting her face while she is outside until she manages to adjust."

"We don't actually know what will happen to a Q'ehazi after long exposure to the air in your world since it has never been tested. In any case, that would certainly be a way to assuage any fears Barylos may have about it," suggested Abbe.

"That is true," agreed Aurora. "I still have some fears for your safety in visiting Barylos, however. It is a long and arduous journey, way to the north of our land and across water."

"I will accompany Charli," Joslyn suddenly announced, with an air of finality. "She needs support, and I am strong and a healer, should she need any help."

Charli felt a sudden glow in her chest like the sun coming out from behind the clouds and displaying rays of light. She gazed at Joslyn with gratitude and appreciation that made her heart swell and her face redden.

"Very well," Aurora agreed. Perhaps the Sovereign had an inkling that her son's suggestion was more than just being helpful and that he and this girl had some special connection that could be nurtured and supported. In any case, she seemed relieved at the idea that Joslyn and Charli would travel together. "Do you wish this, Charli?"

"Oh yes, yes!" Charli felt a strong surge of relief that she would not be traveling alone, along with excitement and anticipation that she would be with the person she most wanted to be with in this world.

"Then you will leave tomorrow. And we will give you all the resources you need for the journey."

Chapter Eleven

When Angela got back from work at the Mission Elementary School that afternoon, she plucked up enough courage to perform the test she'd purchased a couple of days ago. With trembling fingers, she held up the dial to the light to see the results, and a slow smile of wonderment spread over her face— it was positive!

Angela had not wanted to dare hope it was possible, especially this late in the game. She'd been told after having Charli she couldn't get pregnant again, that no more children were possible for her. That was 21 years ago. Yet here she was, at the age of 40, quite possibly pregnant again. How could that be true?

After missing her period last month, the little flutter of hope had been tugging at her chest and she tried to push it down, again and again. Yet all the signs were there. Yes, she'd been feeling more emotional than usual, and she admonished herself for snapping at the misbehaving children in her class. Yes, a couple of times in the past few days she felt nauseous as soon as she woke up and vomited in the sink, thankfully after Bill left for work so he didn't notice. Yes, if she put her hand on her stomach, she could feel the tiniest little bump, and so perhaps she didn't need to dismissed it as imaginary.

If it was really true, this would certainly be a miracle child, and all she'd ever hoped for. She always wanted to have more than one child; in fact, she dreamed of having a big family of loving and boisterous youngsters running around the house. Yet somehow that had never happened for her, so she gave up believing it ever would.

The whole situation with Charli was stressful from the start and it didn't improve. After all, Angela was barely 19, a child herself, when she became pregnant with her daughter. The father was uninterested in participating and, in fact, she completely lost touch with him a few months after Charli's birth. Then her parents disowned her after she married Chuck, Charli's stepdad.

Over the years, her relationship with Charli was always fraught with emotions, especially after Chuck's death and their move to a different state against Charli's wishes. Angela sometimes wondered if Charli still bore a grudge against her for that move, although it was one of many subjects never discussed between them.

Angela had gotten used to Charli's independence and, in her opinion, cavalier attitude toward family. But she still wasn't pleased by it, and the situation wasn't what she'd imagined from an only daughter. The one thing that could assuage all of Angela's disappointments was to have another child, and that possibility, she'd believed, was a closed door for her–until now!

Angela had been so busy navigating the waves of bliss and excitement washing over her at the thought of her new future that she'd forgotten to make the usual preparations for dinner she always did before Bill returned home from work. She glanced at her watch and realized with a jolt that it was almost 5:30 p.m., and she'd have to hurry if she didn't want to be late.

With a burst of frenzied energy, she rushed downstairs to the kitchen and started chopping up vegetables for chicken soup that evening. She told Alexa to play some of her favorite country music, and she sang the songs she knew so loudly that she failed to hear Bill's key in the lock as he entered through the front door a few minutes later.

"Hi, Honey," he announced, striding in and kissing her briefly on the cheek. "You sound like you're in a good mood."

Angela beamed at him, her face aglow with love and excitement. "That's right, I am. I've got something to tell you."

"Hmmm," Bill responded, his lips pursed in surprise. His face expressed the bemusement and acceptance that Angela knew and loved so well. She knew that he was a man who could take anything in stride and support her through any trouble, yet who could also participate in her joy and celebrate her success. Truly, she reflected, she was lucky to have found him at last. She regarded his broad shoulders, his kind brown eyes, and his thick crop of graying hair with fondness, feeling so grateful that this baby was his.

"Okay. I'll just take a quick shower before dinner and you can tell me then," replied Bill, wandering out of the kitchen. Then a thought struck him. "Oh, Hon, I thought you said Charli was coming home. Is she in her room?" he called as he approached the stairs leading to the bedrooms.

Angela put a hand to her mouth in embarrassment, "Oh my God, I can't believe I forgot all about her. I'm not sure if she's joining us for dinner or not. She didn't say." A pang of guilt struck her as she realized how quickly she'd forgotten her first daughter now that a baby was likely on the way.

"Where is she?" inquired Bill. He always expressed a fatherly interest in Charli, even though she was already an adult when he'd met her. Their relationship was cordial, if a little more distant than Angela would have liked. Bill was the sort of warm and approachable person who just about anybody would feel comfortable being around.

Angela walked into the living room so she could talk to Bill more easily. "I'm not sure, to be honest. She got home yesterday afternoon and went to bed early because she was so tired. I didn't want to wake her this morning, and I didn't see her before I went to work. Then when I got home, she wasn't here, so I assumed she'd gone somewhere."

"Oh, well. I'm sure she's fine. Probably gone to visit friends or something. It's great that she's so independent and can take care of herself." Bill always saw the positive side of everything.

"Yes, you're right. I'm not going to worry. She'll be back when she wants to be back. If she wants dinner, she'll have to sort it out for herself."

Bill went upstairs to shower and dress, and Angela returned to her kitchen chores, reflecting on how different her attitude was to her daughter these days, *especially with a potential new addition to the family,* she thought with a grin as she patted her belly once more. In the old days, she'd been over-protective and anxious, always feeling that she was not a good enough mother and had to compensate for some perceived inadequacy. But that was before therapy, and Bill, and this improbable and unexpected development!

Chapter Twelve

They had come to the foot of a very high, snow-capped mountain. It was a beautiful place by the shores of a glassy lake with abundant borders of wildflowers. However, as Charli surveyed the peak ahead of them, she felt a sinking sensation of dread at the thought of attempting that nearly impossible ascent. They didn't exactly have climbing gear with them to propel them up such a rockface, and Charli was inexperienced in rock climbing (although she had enjoyed the "climbing wall" at the local adventure center and regarded herself as fairly athletic).

Joslyn did not seem fazed at the thought of the journey ahead, and Charli used this fact to comfort and reassure herself that they would be successful somehow. Charli asked her companion in thought-words whether anybody had come this far north from Q'ehazi before, and he replied that they had not, but they had some idea about the terrain from past explorers who had visited Q'ehazi from other lands. Joslyn carried with him an old map that had been given to the Q'ehazi people some generations before by travelers who were passing through.

Charli reflected briefly on the experiences they had recently had with the local villagers. The borders of Q'ehazi extended only so far as the last village they had encountered, the Village of the Far Northwest, which had somewhat fewer inhabitants than the usual make-up of a

Q'ehazi village, due to its proximity to the wilderness and the extremely cold temperatures in winter. The climate control that most Q'ehazi inhabitants enjoyed also didn't extend this far north, and so the villagers had to contend with temperature fluctuations that were more akin to those Charli knew from her own world.

Being this far north, the villagers spoke with an unusual accent that was foreign to Charli as it was low and guttural with lots of raspy sounds made in the back of the throat. The villagers, however, were friendly and welcoming. Their faces were round and flat and their eyes small and somewhat slanted, as if they had spent most of their days squinting against the harsh glare of the white snow from their wintry terrain. They wore thick and colorful red, blue, and yellow garments made from the fur and hides of local animals, such as deer and elk. It was common practice to ride horses, as people were far from any other form of transport used by Q'ehazi elsewhere.

Horsemanship was a skill they prided themselves on, and they held regular contests between rival horse experts to see who was the best and the fastest rider, accompanied by boisterously cheering crowds. No prizes were given to the winner other than the fame and glory of being proclaimed the best, and many young riders were tempted to try out for this annual horse-riding contest.

Juvana was a young woman around the same age as Charli when she'd discovered the Q'ehazi. She was the daughter of the generous hosts in this village, and she was preparing herself for this horse-riding contest with a great determination to win. The girl was "fearless and strong" as her father described her proudly, and she wore her long white-blonde hair in a practical ponytail down her back, so that it wouldn't get in the way as she rode and demonstrated her skills.

Juvana loved more than anything to overcome a challenge and to attempt something everybody believed she couldn't accomplish. Therefore, the horse she had chosen for this event was a new mare, a young filly that had not been broken in yet and, in fact, showed a stubbornness and rebelliousness equal to Juvana's own character.

Charli and Joslyn watched in dismay as again and again, Juvana attempted to tame the horse long enough to ride it in the contest, but she was thrown off its back countless times. On each occasion, the girl got up, dusted herself off with a groan of frustration, gritted her teeth, and tried again. But Juvana was starting to realize she was maybe no match for this horse, and the contest was fast approaching.

One day when there were only three days left until the contest, Juvana tried to tame this horse enough to mount and ride on its back, as Charli, Joslyn, and her parents watched with gloomy faces. As usual, Juvana was thrown disrespectfully off the horse's back, and all of the watchers groaned in disappointment. But this time, the girl didn't get up again, not for several minutes, and her audience started to become concerned.

"Juvana, why aren't you getting up?" her mother wailed from the sidelines as her father leapt into the paddock to aid her. Joslyn also ran to the girl, and helped her father carry her to safety until she could recuperate.

"I'm fine, I'm fine," the girl protested, but Charli could see that her face was wan, and her brow was furrowed, and she seemed less sanguine than usual. When Charli's attention was diverted back to the paddock, she was surprised to see that Joslyn had walked over to the horse and was speaking to the animal in a low, gentle voice, barely audible, while stroking its nose. After several minutes of doing this, Charli was amazed to see that the horse followed Joslyn to the side of the paddock with great docility like a well-trained circus beast.

"What did you do to calm it down?" Charli gasped, amazed.

"Nothing really. Spoke to her nicely. She was afraid but she'll be okay now."

True enough, after Juvana rested and felt well enough to revisit the paddock, this time she went in with Joslyn, and he spoke quietly and calmly to the horse as Juvana slowly lifted herself up and on to the horse's back. After a few minutes of riding, the creature seemed to accommodate its new partner, and now Juvana took it out of the paddock and into the open fields where the horse's canter developed into a gallop and they both disappeared into the distance.

Juvana's father grasped Joslyn's hand in both of his own and beamed, "Thank you, young man, whether or not she wins the competition, you have restored my daughter's heart and that makes me very happy."

"No thanks needed," replied Joslyn graciously. "You have been so generous and kind to us, and we appreciate your hospitality. This just goes a little way toward repaying you."

Early the next morning before they set off on their long journey up the side of the mountain, Juvana's mother approached Charli carrying a small leather pouch.

"This is for you," she said as she handed it to the young woman.

"Thank you very much," said Charli, smiling. She held the pouch in her hands and noticed that it gave off an odd and very pungent odor. She didn't like to ask what it was for fear of offending the woman.

"You must always wear it around your neck," said the older woman, placing the pouch on a leather cord around Charli's neck. "It contains powerful healing herbs. You may need them one day."

"Wow, okay, thank you."

Charli and Juvana's mother gave the customary bow that was used both in greeting and departure. As Charli and Joslyn made their way across the fields toward the foot of the mountain, the sight of the villagers receded into the distance and they became smaller and smaller as the air around them became colder and more arid with every step.

The people in the Village of the Far Northwest had been extremely accommodating and welcoming, as well as impressed by the fact that Charli and Joslyn had embarked upon such a dangerous mission, which they had heard was vital to the well-being of Q'ehazi people everywhere. Thus, they were very grateful to the visitors and gave them everything they needed for their journey, including food and supplies, and a welcome respite from the harsh weather that awaited them. Fortunately for Charli and Joslyn, the time of year was spring, and so the temperatures of this part of the world were less inclement than during the winter months. That aided their spirits and their sense of optimism moving forward.

Still, they were venturing into the unknown and that was the scariest part of the experience. Reports of the whereabouts of Barylos and her followers had filtered back to Sovereign Aurora through various channels, and so Charli and Joslyn had an idea of her rough location. Even accounting for the limited map provided to them, Charli knew that the road ahead would not be easy. She knew that once they arrived at the very northwesterly tip of this continent, they would have to cross over a body of water covering a very narrow isthmus of land that was only accessible during certain times of day, and that would be the most dangerous part of their journey.

Still, where they were was incredibly beautiful, and Charli decided to just relax and enjoy the beauty of the moment and the location. It was around 5:00 p.m. and they had been walking all day. The Q'ehazi conveyor belt ended at the previous village, and now the only option for their transport was to walk. Fortunately, they had both been furnished with strong hiking boots and warm clothes for their journey, plus their hiking backpacks contained a comfortable tent and plenty of provisions that they could carry between them.

Joslyn began to pitch the tent and, with Charli's help, they managed to erect the structure in about 15 minutes. Then they began preparing their rough dinner cooked on a small portable stove and eaten on sturdy metal plates. Charli had not done much wilderness camping before in her young life, but she took to the experience right away and recognized she possessed a strong streak of resourcefulness and practicality that she'd never had to use before.

The only time Charli had ever done anything like this was a few years before her father died, when Daddy had taken her on a trip to Yosemite National Park. They spent the day hiking and the evening camping out in a tent. That was a vacation Charli's mother had not attended, as Angela was much less inclined to spend time outside in nature than her daughter. It had been a wonderful bonding experience for Charli who learned to adore and revere her father even more during that trip.

Even though Joslyn was nothing like her father in many ways, something about his masculine energy and his practical ability to master the business at hand comforted and inspired Charli. Her father had been sociable and garrulous, whereas Joslyn was quiet and reserved, but they both had an inner strength about them and a resilience that Charli admired and wished to emulate. Chuck Speranza had been a successful corporate executive who charmed people with his handsome face and charismatic personality.

Joslyn, by contrast, was more the Q'ehazi embodiment of "successful" as he had attained a *State of Grace* relatively early in his life, and his values of caring and generosity were much embraced by his family and societal culture. They were both men of their times and their societies, which were widely different and yet they had similarities, too. Being honest and dependable was important to them; sensitivity was not seen as weakness; and creativity was valuable and could come in many forms. Charli reflected on these similarities and wondered, Why did she feel so drawn to Joslyn and so comfortable in his presence?

Their relationship up until that point had been like that of a brother and sister. Although they occupied one tent, they had separate sleeping bags, and they slept fully clothed in their night gear. Charli had never had a brother, and this familial bond was new to her, but it was also strangely natural and pleasant. Perhaps Joslyn regarded her as Abbe's friend first and foremost, and that is why he'd slipped into this fraternal role with her. In any case, their relationship had deepened, but was still on a friendship level, with any romantic intentions being left unspoken.

Charli didn't know much about Joslyn's prior romantic attachments (apart from what his sister had briefly alluded to), and she didn't like to pry by asking about them, especially as he was a private person. Therefore, their conversations tended to stick to practical aspects of what they were aiming to accomplish, and occasionally to stray into more general themes, such as Joslyn illuminating the aspects of Q'ehazi life for Charli that she had not known about before.

Charli was amazed to discover, for instance, that all business entities in Q'ehazi were run as cooperatives, meaning that there were no bosses or employees, and any profits were automatically plowed back into the company or distributed equally among all people involved. Joslyn was similarly amazed when Charli admitted to him that no such equality existed in her world, and that for most people, money was something that was supposed to make life easier and yet made life more difficult and complicated for the vast majority of the population.

When they had finished their dinner, the day was starting to turn to dusk, and they both sat in silence, regarding the gorgeous sunset displayed over the edge of the mountain range, taking in the sounds of the gentle lapping of water against the shores of the lake, and the evening cicadas starting to sing their constant chorus. They were sniffing the air scented with trees and flowers and tasting the warm cinnamon and honey in their evening mugs of milk.

Once it was fully dark, but before retiring for the night, they enjoyed the canopy of stars that appeared above them, and talked in thought-words about which stars were in the sky and what planet or constellation they represented. Charli had always loved star-gazing, and that was another interest she had shared with her father. In this moment, the dangers ahead of them and her apprehensions evaporated as she enjoyed the opportunity to share this special bonding moment with a man she was beginning to know and like more as their friendship became deeper and more secure.

Chapter Thirteen

When she initially heard the sound, the darkness around them prevented Charli from deciding if her eyes were open or closed. A low growl, very quiet at first, so that Charli wondered if she'd really heard something or if she'd just awakened from a dream. But then she heard it again, a little louder and quite close. She strained her eyes to see in the gloom, and once they adjusted, she could almost make out the contours of the tent with its gray folds being the only thing that separated her and Joslyn from the outside. She remembered that the tent material was a flimsy fabric, just as she noticed a distinct movement in the folds at the front of the tent accompanied by a definite guttural animal sound, and she sat bolt upright in her sleeping bag with a sharp gasp of alarm.

"Joslyn, Joslyn!" she exclaimed in a low but urgent whisper as she jostled him awake in the neighboring sleeping bag. "I think something is outside the tent!"

Joslyn woke immediately and quickly got out of his sleeping bag. He wore his sleeping clothes of loose-fitting pants and a t-shirt.

"Don't move," he warned her in thought-words, "and try not to make a sound." His body was still but intensely focused as he listened for more animal noises until another low growl signaled that the animal, whatever it was, was outside of the tent and intended to come inside.

"It must be a golden bear," he told her in thought-words, "Fortunately not a black bear or a grizzly. I've heard they have them here. They are mostly gentle creatures unless the females are protecting their cubs or they are looking for food."

"You mean us?" Charli asked in horrified thought-words.

"Not necessarily. Any food. They are usually still in hibernation at this time. It must be an old bear who didn't get enough food to last through the winter. Maybe it smelled our dinner last night. We should have been more careful when we were cooking outside."

Charli tensed her body in anticipation of what was to come, feeling a drop in the pit of her stomach at the realization that they were in more danger than they realized.

"What can we do?"

"Stay alert. I have a club in my bag. Just have to reach for it." There was another violent movement of the tent from outside. This time there could be no mistaking that the bear was trying to shake their tent and maybe intended to attack.

Charli was trying to control her trembling and the powerful beating of her heart that was so loud she was surprised the bear didn't hear it.

Joslyn fumbled in his bag for his club, which was difficult to locate in the penetrating gloom, but eventually he found it and held it aloft in preparation for what he knew was coming.

"Stay back," he instructed her.

"What, you're not going out there?"

"Yes. As soon as you are able, get out of the tent and run for cover. Anything you can find behind rocks or trees."

"Up a tree?"

"Yes, but remember, bears are often good climbers, too."

"Oh, God!"

"You'll be okay, you'll be okay," reassured Joslyn, but Charli picked up the fear behind his soothing thought-words and knew that he was going to do all he could, but it might not be enough.

What came next was blurred in Charli's memory when she thought of it later because it happened so fast and was so confusing. A much louder animal sound made Joslyn rip open the tent's door and lunge outside. Charli darted out of the tent and fled to a nearby tree where she watched what was happening from her safe place behind its trunk. She watched with consternation as Joslyn and the bear fought, and Joslyn pounded the enraged animal, which appeared even in the gloom to be almost twice his size and weighed a ton at least. Charli clung to the tree in trembling horror as she saw the bear mauling her beloved Joslyn with its huge paws and wrestling him to the ground.

Seeing the blood oozing from deep gashes in Joslyn's face, she couldn't wait any longer, and with a piercing cry, she grabbed a large log and ran up to the bear and hit it. Stunned and confused, the bear responded to the blows on its back by turning and facing Charli, and she realized with horror that she had placed herself in harm's way in front of a huge and angry bear who was wounded and in pain. As the bear moved toward her snarling in pain and fury, Charli was on the brink of accepting her fate as a dead woman when suddenly the animal collapsed on its side and moaned in agony. Joslyn had stood up and landed the fatal blow on the animal's side and then pummeled it with more blows until it fell.

Charli was shaking like a leaf with tears streaming down her dirt-stained face as she stumbled to stand up. She watched as the bear gave a dying gasp and then lay motionless. All the life was finally knocked out of it. She saw Joslyn dropping the club and falling to his knees beside the bear and burying his head in his hands. "I'm sorry, I'm sorry," he appeared to be sobbing.

Charli shakily approached him. She noticed the club was covered in blood and matted fur. Her emotions were a mix of shock, fear and intense sadness as she gently stroked Joslyn's back with her hand. She laid her head on his shoulder, and they both stayed that way for a few minutes. Eventually, his weeping subsided, and he started to straighten his back. Charli stretched up and gazed at him, her look both tender and grateful.

"You saved me," she said aloud.

"You saved me, too," he responded, also aloud. The sound of their voices seemed odd in the gloom, more like an echo than a real sound, cracked with strain and emotion.

Charli was still breathing heavily. "Why were you crying?"

"The bear was only looking for food. It didn't deserve to die. I had to save us. I wish, I wish…." his voice faltered out of words.

"I understand," said Charli. "It wasn't intentional. We had to defend ourselves."

Joslyn nodded in miserable assent. "I've never killed anything before," he admitted.

"Neither have I."

"Don't people in your world kill all the time?"

"No, not *all* the time. Not *all* of us. But in self-defense, of course." Charli smiled weakly.

"I guess I've given you a terrible impression of us, haven't I?"

Joslyn didn't answer and smiled back.

"We cannot bury him as we cannot lift him. But I would like to wash my club in the creek, and we can do a small ceremony to honor his passing."

"Okay," Charli assented. "But first we need to treat your wounds."

Charli was still wearing the pouch from Juvana's mother around her neck. It contained an ointment that was good for quickly healing wounds. What a blessing it was that she always carried this pouch with her.

While they sat by the creek, Charli took some soft grasses and gently wiped away the dried blood from Joslyn's face before applying the ointment. She'd never done anything like this, but it came naturally to her, and she felt glad to help in this way.

Then as the first fingers of daylight started to salute the morning, Joslyn sang a mournful song and prayed over the body of the dead bear, thanking the Great One for letting them live, and asking that the animal be conveyed in spirit form to the World Above, and be transmuted into stardust again, ready to return to this planet in another form when his time came once more.

Charli had never attended anything so magical and strangely uplifting as this simple ceremony that honored the taking of one life and the saving of another. She recognized in that moment, the connection of all life and all living forms of life on this planet and beyond. She was grateful for the hundredth time that she'd been given this opportunity to spend her life with these people who were connected to all of Nature in such a simple yet complete manner.

The golden bear incident was terrifying, and yet looking back, it wasn't even the most difficult part of their journey—that still awaited them.

For three days, Charli and Joslyn journeyed to the top of the mountain that looked so monumental when gazing at it from the valley floor. The mountain looked even more imposing, while attempting to climb up its almost sheer face to the top. Many times, as they staggered up the peak, sometimes clambering up steep portions, sometimes stumbling over a rocky yet more level platform, Charli looked up, hoping to see that they were at least a little closer to the top. Yet she was always disappointed to see that they were not much closer to the summit than when they started. The mountain still stretched before them, sternly commanding the landscape in its vastness, and teasing them as if to say, "You will never conquer me, I am too big and too high for you tiny humans." But they persisted. No choice but to continue. They could not turn back now, having come this far. Plus, their mission was too important to abandon.

The icy cold with its biting wind, chilled Charli to her bones. All her extremities felt numb and lifeless; her breath formed crystals in front of her face at every exhale; she felt disconnected from her body, as it ascended into the icy vastness of the mountain, with only her willpower to urge her on. It took all of her concentration to take one step in front of the next, and she imagined Joslyn must feel the same way. Their communication as they climbed was minimal as they needed to conserve all of their strength for the ascent.

At the end of each day, they huddled in their tent, sharing one sleeping bag and using their combined body warmth to protect them from the cold. There was a closeness now between them that was unspoken and yet perceptible, the bond formed by undergoing a traumatic event with another person that needed no words to explain or embellish it.

On the evening of the second day of hiking up the mountain, after they'd pitched the tent and huddled inside it to stay as warm as possible, Charli tried to remove her shoes and socks. She realized that her feet were completely numb after several hours of walking. After peeling off the socks with difficulty, Charli and Joslyn saw that her toes were completely blue. Joslyn attempted to warm her feet with both of his hands, and eventually their natural color and feeling came back. Joslyn put her shoes and socks by the fire to dry them. The fire also kept animals at bay. The next morning, Charli was reluctant to wear her socks and shoes but she knew she had to wear them to complete the journey.

At around midday on the third day, they reached the top of the mountain and stood on a small crest overlooking the land. They were impressed at how far they had come. Charli was surprised she didn't feel any sense of triumph or accomplishment, just a weary finality at having reached this moment.

As they surveyed the vista, they saw that the land ended abruptly past the valley floor, and a large body of water separated them from the next continent. They made out the shores of the other land to the west barely beyond the horizon with its faint line indicating the water's edge. Joslyn explained that this was the isthmus that separated the two continents and that the water receded once a day, allowing enough hours to cross the narrow passage before the tide covered it with water. They had to time their crossing very carefully to avoid being swept away by the ocean currents. It was also treacherous because this tidal opportunity came as dusk descended, so it would be almost dark by the time they reached the other shore. At least they knew what they had to do and when they had to do it.

The descent from the mountain was faster than the ascent, and they reached the valley floor by around 4:00 p.m. the next day. They had about three good hours of springtime daylight to catch the receding tide and cross the land before the rising tide.

It was a beautiful spring day, and Joslyn and Charli were grateful for the sun's warmth as they walked across the last strand before the water's edge. They took a little time to rest, recuperate, and eat before the final leg of their journey. Although they later regretted their decision, at this juncture, they needed to experience small joys such as the warm sunlight and peeling off some of the clothing that protected them from the icy winds on top of the mountain.

They picked up their bags and stepped onto the narrow strip of land that joined two continents. Joslyn and Charli experienced sensations of lightness and optimism for the first time in several days, and these felt good. They saw the distant hazy line of the other continent because they had surveyed it from the top of the mountain. They knew the distance to cross was around five miles, and the time required was one hour—a relatively easy feat at 5:00 p.m. with two hours of daylight before high tide.

Charli changed her heavy hiking boots for lighter walking shoes for this part of the journey. Joslyn was walking a few steps ahead of her, and both of them were walking quickly across the rocky ground. Charli was looking at the horizon and the water to both sides, her mind daydreaming and visualizing the future.

She thought of the time when she and Joslyn would successfully return to Q'ehazi, hopefully accompanied by Barylos and her army that she persuaded as planned to follow her to the portal and into her world. Charli had not thought much beyond this plan because it was overwhelming and almost unimaginable. But if she could accomplish this mission, if only she *could*, there was no telling what wonderful options would emerge for her.

Perhaps because she was daydreaming and not concentrating on the rocky ground and keeping her steps sure and strong, or perhaps because she was wearing new and unfamiliar shoes, what happened next was so shocking and unexpected that she was knocked off her feet.

Suddenly, Charli felt something like a rock hit her left calf, and she screamed and fell to her knees. Joslyn heard her scream and ran to her. "What happened?"

"I don't know," she cried, unable to stop her tears. "Ow, it hurts, it really hurts!"

"It's okay, you'll be okay," Joslyn soothed her. "We'll use the ointments in your pouch and I've got bandages in my bag."

Charli sat on the rocky ground and breathed heavily.

"I don't understand it," she said. "I was just walking."

"Where did whatever hit you come from?"

Charli looked around and did not see anyone.

"I don't know. It felt like somebody threw a rock at me, but there's nobody. Really weird."

"Did you stumble on a rock?"

"I don't know."

Unable to explain the mystery, Joslyn concentrated on Charli's wound and applied ointment and then bandaged her leg as best he could. She had a deep gash and a large purple bruise started to spread across her skin.

"Can you stand up?"

"I think so." Charli winced in pain as she hobbled along.

"What about walking? I think we've got a couple of miles to go."

Charli was determined not to show weakness or to jeopardize the trip across the land. "I'm okay. I'll be fine."

Joslyn set out ahead of her and glanced back at her frequently to check on her condition and whereabouts.

Charli was not fine and every step was agony on her damaged leg, but she gritted her teeth and made her way across the ground, determined to cross before nightfall. Walking two miles on her now very painful leg was too difficult to contemplate, so she hummed a cheerful tune and tried valiantly to reflect on other things so she could carry on. She had run races in her sprinting days, and she knew that the best way to win a race was to not think about the finish line but to focus on getting to the next goalpost.

Joslyn had the great good fortune of finding a fallen tree branch among the rocks on the road, and he took it and created a sturdy walking stick for Charli, as she hobbled along on her wounded leg.

About 6:45 p.m., shortly before dusk gave way to darkness and the ocean closed in on the isthmus separating the continents, Charli gave up trying to calculate how much farther she had to walk. Joslyn had already reached the narrow tip of the continent and turned to aid Charli. They both saw the water presently lapping at the edges of the isthmus, making the strip of land narrower every minute.

"Come on, you can do it, you can," encouraged Joslyn, as he grabbed Charli by the waist and carried her across the ground.

"Okay, I can do it. I can," responded Charli whose determination belied her inner trepidation and uncertainty.

Joslyn had already taken both of their bags to the other side about 100 yards away.

"Should I carry you?"

Charli's pride got the better of her. "No, it's okay. I can do it."

The water was so close, only a few inches of land to walk on, and her shoes were getting wet.

"Don't be proud," urged Joslyn. "Jump on my back."

Charli obeyed, and he took slow steps across the tiny strip of land. The ocean was a few inches deep, so he plunged through the water, hoping to get to the other shore before it got too deep.

"Can you swim?" he yelled to Charli, after realizing swimming might be their only option.

"Yes, I'm quite a good swimmer."

The cold ocean water rose up to Joslyn's chest.

"Hold onto my back," he prompted. "I'm going to swim the last few yards to shore."

Charli tried to obey his instruction, but the fierce current was pulling them apart. Although Charli strained to hold onto Joslyn's back, she felt her hands slipping. The salt water stung her eyes, but Joslyn was swimming with strength and vigor. She prayed that he would make it to shore and that she could hold on for a few more moments. She'd never been so terrified, not even when the bear was attacking them, because that all happened and ended quickly. Her strength to hold on was ebbing, and she was gasping for breath.

Then suddenly a huge wave crashed over Charli's back and she screamed. As she bobbed up above the ocean, she yelled for help and saw Joslyn in front of her, desperately trying to reach her across the waves.

She felt mind-numbing terror, and all she could think about was survival. She was gasping for air and flailing desperately to stay above the water long enough to breathe. She tried to calm her hysteria, realizing that panic would only make things worse. She had one focus: stay above the water.

The ocean and its currents were too powerful for her—a tiny speck in this vast sea—and she was being sucked down into the icy cavernous depths. Her energy started to ebb, but her will to survive stayed strong. Then her legs felt weak and powerless, especially with her injury.

To Charli's great relief, she felt Joslyn grab her arm and pull her. She saw him ahead of her splashing his legs through the water.

All in a rush, they crashed onto the rocky shore of the other side and lay panting, almost unable to realize that they had survived.

Chapter Fourteen

Abbe loved this time of day and often spent it with her father fly-fishing for trout in the local creek. The sun dipped below the horizon, and the sky glowed pink with golden shadows cast by the streaking clouds. The air was still and warm, and a soft breeze permeated the calmness, gradually ruffling Abbe's hair into soft tufts that framed her face momentarily. She heard the soft swish, swish of Serano's rod as he expertly skimmed the water hunting for the elusive fish.

He was a quiet man, and yet when he felt a fish tug on his line, he let out a whoop of joy and waded out into the water to pull it out and free it from the line.

"What a beauty!" Abbe exclaimed in thought-words.

Serano beamed at her and sent his grateful message, "We will have an abundance to eat tonight." He came up to his daughter and squeezed her shoulders in his strong arms. "Tonight, we celebrate abundance and we cast away sadness.

"Sadness?" queried Abbe.

"I see it in your eyes. I know you miss your brother, and you worry about him and Charli on their long journey."

"It's just that I wish we could project our thoughts further than a few feet. It's terrible not knowing how or where they are. I've even tried to contact them in my dreams, but no success." Abbe couldn't help a mournful pursing of her lips at this recollection.

"I have faith they will be back in time."

"Now you sound like mother," Abbe quipped.

"Well, she is a wise woman, the wisest I ever met."

Serano put the fish in his basket with the others from their day.

"Come, daughter, let's return to the village and show the others our catch today. We've done well—you in particular. Look at the trout you caught. I'm proud of you."

"Yes, I am finally learning how to do it. Must be all those years of watching you."

Abbe lifted the heavy basket and followed her father as he trudged along the path to the village where the evening's festivities were planned.

Abbe loved attending the Story Evening when all the villagers participated in some way. After dinner with everyone seated in a circle on the ground around a large and warming fire, each participant shared something creative: a story that inspired others by demonstrating *Acts of Grace*, either real or fictional, in order for listeners to learn "good behavior"; a beautiful work of art, such as a rock painting or a wonderfully crafted basket; a song or musical melody that everyone knew and could share; or a dance also made for sharing. Nobody was excluded from this activity, and all were celebrated and enjoyed. Abbe shared a musical piece she had recently learned on her violin.

At the same time as her daughter and husband were walking back to the village after fishing in the creek, Sovereign Aurora sat cross-legged in the center of her prayer labyrinth. It being the evening of the full moon, she had come to meditate and ponder. Many of her recent hours were spent in solitary reflection in this way. The burden of responsibility weighed heavily upon her. She had been chosen as leader of the Q'ehazi people because she had attained a *State of Grace* relatively early in life, but for the first time she was beginning to question her abilities.

Aurora wished she could have helped Barylos and stopped the plague that attacked their people. She reflected on how *The Great Sickness* infected them not only physically but also mentally and emotionally as a sickness of distrust and disharmony. That little flame from Sean had ignited in Barylos what was there already like dry wood waiting to be lit. The fire was lit by *The Great Sickness* that pervaded the land and caused the death of Maudina and so many others. Aurora felt compassion for Barylos, despite everything she had suffered at the hands of her daughter, but she knew she could not allow that fire to consume her people because they were her children and she was responsible for all of them.

Barylos needed to be sent to a place from which she could never return, so she no longer posed a threat to the Q'ehazi people. When Charli suggested leading Barylos back to her world, that sounded like the perfect solution. Aurora still wondered, *Was it was really the right thing to do, to send her daughter away to a place she knew nothing about?*

Although Barylos had rejected the Q'ehazi ways and culture, and Aurora had therefore no regrets about commanding her to leave, the girl was still her daughter and her responsibility. Barylos had always been stubborn and wayward and difficult to manage. Yet she was still worthy of love as all children are. Aurora searched in her heart to see if she had loved her any less than her other children or treated her differently. Perhaps that was the reason this daughter had turned so completely against her mother and everything the sovereign stood for.

Aurora felt compassion for her daughter. *Had Barylos felt subtly neglected or abandoned?* She'd always been different, but did that come first or was it that she'd never felt that sense of belonging and therefore had rejected others as she herself felt rejected and excluded?

Aurora had a powerful recollection of a time when Barylos was 10 years old and they were playing the Q'ehazi game "Everybody Wins" with 20 children and extended family members. As usual, everybody was happy to play the game collaboratively and allow every participant to become a winner in some way. Nobody was left out. But Barylos did not favor that outcome. Even though nobody had taught her, she insisted on playing the game competitively and winning everything for herself. This meant other individuals lost and received nothing.

From that day on, there was a subtle distrust of this girl among other people of the village, Sovereign Aurora could feel this distrust and couldn't dismiss it. She spoke up for her daughter and tried to defend her by asserting that she was young and didn't realize the value of collaboration. Barylos had often gone off on her own rather than playing with the other children. One time, Aurora had caught her throwing stones at a badger and laughing at the animal's pain and discomfort.

Barylos' father, Gallo, was a white man from a distant village who swept Aurora off her feet when she was very young and before she became the Sovereign. Then when their baby was barely two years old, he disappeared one day for no apparent reason never to be seen again. Aurora suffered greatly at this time, and her suffering was one of the things that gave her such compassion for others who suffered. Her forgiveness of Gallo for his betrayal was one of the indicators of her *State of Grace*.

Little Barylos was the spitting image of her father, and Aurora couldn't help but see Gallo's face in her young daughter. After meeting Serano and having two children with him, Aurora made every attempt to treat all her children fairly and equally, but maybe she hadn't completely succeeded. Maybe Gallo's physical appearance wasn't the only thing Barylos inherited from her father. *There is only so much I can teach a child,* Aurora reflected, and beyond that, the child had its own nature and would go its own way eventually. Joslyn and Abbe were such blessings that maybe Aurora had focused more attention on them than on her eldest daughter and Barylos felt deprived.

It was almost sunset and Aurora realized it was later than she thought. She rose to her feet and shivered from a nearby breeze. That evening a feast and a festival would be attended not only by people from her village but also by people from the Village of the Sorrowful. These people were sick or damaged and were tended to by caregivers, who sometimes brought them to celebrations and festivities.

Aurora scheduled visits to their village at least weekly, and this was an extra bonus activity for them. Aurora loved more than anything to spread joy as she believed it was her life's work.

Artists, dancers, and musicians from nearby villages gave impromptu performances and encouraged all audience members to participate, including the Sorrowful Villagers.

After the festivities concluded, the Sovereign named a new Elder for her village. Elders were always chosen by the Sovereign as helpful surrogates who carried out many of her duties so she was not overly burdened by all her responsibilities as the leader. Aurora offered advice and support to anybody who wanted or needed it, and she fulfilled the obligations of a therapist, judge, and government official, all rolled into one. Her work was such a monumental task that no one could successfully fulfill all of it, and thus the Sovereign regularly chose others who demonstrated they could carry out her responsibilities without much guidance from her. The Elder she was naming this evening was an older man who had seen many tragedies in his life and had borne his pain with wisdom and acceptance, which were qualities that Aurora admired. She knew his empathy and compassion would be very helpful to him in carrying out his duties.

Aurora walked swiftly back to the road, passing farmers working in the fields harvesting vegetables, and she exchanged a friendly nod and a wave with them. When she arrived at the road, she hopped on to the moving transport belt as it was some distance to the place where they were dining that night and she didn't want to be late. She smiled and said hello to the other people she met along the way, all of whom knew or recognized her. It wasn't their custom to be deferential to the Sovereign, but their love and respect for her was genuine and freely expressed.

Chapter Fifteen

Charli and Joslyn arrived at a province that was different from anywhere they had been before. Even in her own world, Charli mused, this landscape would have been barren, hostile, and unforgiving. They perched on a rock face overlooking a valley. Charli was glad of this brief respite, as her leg was still throbbing in pain. She laid on the ground and Joslyn knelt beside her to look at the vista and search for any clues of habitation. The ground was hard and dry. The air was cold and stung her face. The sky was a steely uncompromising gray. The vast plains stretched out before them unbroken by a single tree or landmark with no evidence of human civilization.

"Are you sure this is the right place?" Charli pondered aloud. "There doesn't seem to be anybody here at all."

Before Joslyn could respond, they heard a loud crack that startled them. Joslyn swung around and Charli staggered to her feet. When she turned around, she was shocked to see three men wearing Khaki battle gear and clutching rifles. The man in the middle fumed, "Who are you and what do you want here?" He pointed his gun directly at them in a threatening gesture.

"We are looking for Barylos," Joslyn announced confidently. Charli tried to stand as tall as she could and to stop her damaged leg from wobbling as the three uniformed men with weapons formed a wall in front of them.

"Who are you? What do you want with Barylos?" barked the middleman again.

"We are Joslyn and Charli from Q'ehazi."

"From Q'ehazi?" the man repeated skeptically. "Search them for weapons," he ordered one of his men.

When the man approached Charli and started patting her down roughly, she lost her balance and collapsed with a small scream.

"Hey, she's hurt," shouted Joslyn urgently, trying to help Charli to stand up again, but the man was in his way.

"Keep back," ordered the man with the gun still pointed at them.

"We don't have any weapons. Leave her alone," urged Joslyn.

The man continued to pluck at Charli's clothes, as she squirmed away from him as much as she could while still complying with being searched.

"Shut up!" commanded the man with the gun. "Do you want to get shot?"

The soldier who'd been ordered to search Charli gave up on her and turned to Joslyn, but he didn't find anything. Eventually, he returned to his position alongside his superior officer.

"We're going to have to take you in," announced the lead soldier.

"What do you mean?" Charli trembled.

"We don't allow people to wander around in our territory. You must come with us. We'll take you to Barylos."

Charli and Joslyn were roughly bundled into a strange-looking metal contraption unlike anything Charli had ever seen. This was obviously their mode of transport operated by an engine like an automobile, except that it was noisy and slow.

To their chagrin, Charli and Joslyn were blindfolded and hustled into this transport vehicle. Cold, scared, and unable to see where they were going, the two friends held hands to calm each other as they were taken to Barylos' camp or somewhere else. No spoken words or thought-words passed between them, just an occasional squeeze of their hands to show each other that they were hoping for the best outcome.

Charli realized the stark difference between these followers of Barylos and the Q'ehazi people who lived in the same "world" but in vastly different aspects of it. Instead of welcoming smiles and hugs and embrace of strangers with communication on the psychic plane, these people resembled those of her world but of the worst kind. They greeted strangers with suspicion rather than kindness, and their first instinct was to attack and control.

Charli felt certain that they were more like people her world than in the world of the Q'ehazi, and therefore she should take them through the portal. She prayed that she could convince them of the benefits of taking this action.

An hour or two later, the two friends were thrown into separate cells. Their blindfolds were withdrawn and replaced by handcuffs that attached them to the rough stone walls of each cell. Charli wasn't even sure if Joslyn's cell was close to her own as she couldn't hear anything above the cacophony of guards and soldiers milling about outside. Her cell smelled stale and dank, and the air was cold and unforgiving. The soldiers took her bag and left her to shiver in her clothes still damp after being in the water. She touched her wounded leg and tried to be calm with thoughts of the future when perhaps they would meet with Barylos.

How they were being treated made it difficult for them to remain optimistic, but Charli retained a fervent hope that a face-to-face meeting with the Sovereign's daughter would prove fruitful. Charli recognized that Barylos always regarded her as a threat, but Charli had ambitions to dispel that summation of her and to use all of her charm to worm her way into Barylos' favor by appealing to her ego and her lust for power.

Charli had a certain perceptiveness about people that was unusual for a person of her age, which was the main reason that had led her to pursue a career as a psychologist. She believed that if she got close to Barylos and talked to her confidentially, she'd make a good impression. After all, Barylos was a young woman, too—one with ambition and drive and a desire to prove herself—so in some ways they weren't all that different. Perhaps Barylos would disapprove of the way in which the guards and soldiers had treated Charli and Joslyn, who was, after all, her brother. All Charli could do was wait and pray.

Charli didn't know how much time passed or what time it was, as little light came through the tiny windows of her cell. But she heard the guards' voices very nearby and then heard the keys clinking in her cell door. She saw someone, another man dressed in khakis who she had not seen before.

"You can come out now," he stated in a rough voice as he hustled her to her feet and man-handled her out of the door. Charli limped on her wounded leg and moved as fast as she could. In a few moments, they were outside, and she was relieved to see that it was daylight, possibly the next morning. The air was cold and windy as the man ushered her into another larger building that housed a huge open hall with a throng of people. Charli strained to see Joslyn in the crowd, but she didn't recognize anyone.

Charli was pushed to the front of the auditorium and up to a small dais where she was grateful to sit on a stool. Her leg was throbbing and she felt a powerful need to sit down. She felt relieved when she saw Joslyn being pushed and shoved up to the dais to accompany her. When he saw her, he smiled weakly, and his thought-words struggled to say something encouraging. "We're here together. It's going to be okay."

Joslyn was pushed onto the stool next to Charli, and they gazed at each other and held each other's hands. His was cold, and Charli tried to warm it between her hands as she smiled her most hopeful smile.

Charli and Joslyn turned to see the hubbub from the back of the hall that was causing the commotion. They spotted Barylos making her way toward them surrounded by an entourage of soldiers and guards who formed a protective ring around her. Charli had not seen Barylos in five years, but she was still recognizable with her stern face and straight black hair pulled back into a bun. Charli was surprised to see that Barylos wore a soldier's khaki uniform very similar to that of her men. No glamor or pomp and ceremony for her.

Although she saw them, Barylos said nothing as she approached and walked up a few steps to a large chair placed much higher than the others and to the left of them. The conversation among the soldiers quietened and a hush descended upon the hall as everyone waited for Barylos, the leader, to speak.

"So, Miss Charlotte Grace," she sneered as she gave Charli a contemptuous gaze, "you look a little bedraggled. Did you have an accident?" A titter came from the back of the hall.

"Yes, a rock hit me as I was, as we were crossing the isthmus," Charli replied in a small voice that still echoed around the cavernous room.

"What, a rock just leapt out and hit you?" Barylos replied incredulously. Charli nodded. "Did anyone here throw a rock at this poor girl?" Barylos called out sardonically, her question being greeted by more titters and outright jeers. "Are you accident prone or something?"

"No, not usually," Charli responded honestly. "I don't know what happened."

Barylos turned her attention to Charli's companion.

"Joslyn, little brother, what are you doing here? Are you Charlotte Grace's consort?" She expressed the word with as much ire as she could.

Joslyn responded truthfully with a stoic expression that betrayed none of his trepidation.

"I accompanied Charli on her journey. We knew it would be difficult and dangerous, and we wanted her to be safe and not to have to undergo those perils alone." Joslyn's voice was warm and resonant.

In that moment, Charli thought it was strange to hear his voice speaking aloud as she was so familiar with the thought-words that were his usual form of communication. Here, it seemed, there were no thought-words, and people spoke loudly and aggressively.

"So, is the 'we' you speak of you and Aurora?" Barylos spoke her mother's name as if it was difficult for her to say.

"Yes. Sovereign Aurora wanted Charli to be protected."

"How is my mother?" Barylos spat out the last word as if it was an insult.

Joslyn took a moment before responding. "As you know, Sovereign Aurora is not happy with the way things have turned out. She did not wish to expel you from Q'ehazi, but you made it impossible for her not to do so."

"So, she sent this girl in her stead? How very courageous," Barylos said, her voice loaded with sarcasm.

"I wanted to come," Charli piped up. "It was my idea."

Barylos was surprised by this comment, and she descended from her thronelike chair and walked down the steps to confront Charli on her stool.

"What was your intention? For me and mother to be friends again?"

Charli stuttered and didn't get her words out before Barylos interrupted her.

"You'll have to forget about your mission, little girl. My mother and I will never be friends again. You know why? It's all because of you!"

"Me? Why?"

"You killed Maudina!" Barylos yelled in Charli's face. "Maudina was the best woman I ever knew, and you killed her!"

"What do you mean? I never did anything to Maudina. I loved her too!"

"You came from your world, and you brought *The Great Sickness* that killed people. She was the first person to die. There were many others, but she was the first."

"I didn't bring the virus."

Charli had so much more to say, but the words stuck in her throat.

"No, but you brought the man who had *The Great Sickness*, and he infected others in Q'ehazi who then infected others."

"No, no, I didn't bring him. I didn't know he would come. He followed me. I didn't ask him to come. He followed me into Q'ehazi."

"No matter if you intended it or not, that's what happened and you are responsible."

"She can't be held responsible for another person's actions," spoke Joslyn, trying to defend his friend.

Loud boos and jeers from the crowd accompanied Joslyn's comment. Barylos quietened them with a hand gesture. She said her next words quietly with great venom, "I should just kill you both. I don't know why you're not dead already."

Charli's terror and shock at this comment stifled the words she had planned to say. All hope and optimism vanished in that moment. Joslyn was also too stunned to speak.

Sensing their despair, Barylos turned away with a flick of her hand. "Take them away. Get them out of my sight and dispose of them however you wish," she commanded the nearest soldier who then grabbed Charli by the shoulders and prepared to hoist her from the stool.

Joslyn shouted in desperation, "No, wait, wait, she has a proposal. She has an idea! Please just hear her!"

Charli joined him, her voice high and frenzied with fear, "Please let me speak. Let me tell you what I came to say!"

"What should I do, Queen Barylos?" asked the soldier who had Charli's arms firmly pinned behind her back while his companion restrained Joslyn.

Barylos swiveled around to face Charli and her countenance soften a little. "You have an idea, you say? Let's hear it."

Charli was out of breath trying to stand on her damaged leg. "Can I please sit again?" she begged.

Barylos stared at Charli for a long time, gazing at her with an intense focus as if looking at a creature with which she was unfamiliar or a new specimen under a microscope. Barylos was trying to divine Charli's real motives, and she wasn't quite sure whether or not to trust the girl who was her competitor all these years and who was now in a vulnerable state and completely at her mercy. Barylos felt an impulse to gloat and revel in her comparative power, and yet she also recognized the value in listening to Charli's proposal, whatever it might be. She could always exact her revenge later.

Barylos gave a curt nod to the soldier, "Yes." The soldier let Charli go and the girl sat down on the stool and Joslyn sat next to her.

"I didn't come here to try and make you be friends with your mother. I know you are angry with your mother and me. You have the right to be angry."

Charli noticed that Barylos' posture straightened as she listened to this confession.

"Go on," she urged.

"It's true that I brought harm to Q'ehazi, even though that was the last thing I ever wanted. Because of me, Sean followed me to Q'ehazi and brought the virus, *The Great Sickness,* that killed people, many people, and I'm sorry, *so* sorry."

Barylos remained unmoved by Charli's genuine contrition, and her face was a stoical mask. Joslyn's expression was a puzzled frown, as if he was unsure of the way Charli was attempting to explain herself.

Charli struggled on. "I know I did wrong and that caused Maudina to die, but there is a way I can make it up to you."

"How?" Perhaps Barylos was intrigued by this, but Charli couldn't tell yet.

"I know that in your world you have been rejected by the Q'ehazi. They don't understand what a great leader you could be."

There was agreement in Barylos' eyes, although she said nothing.

"In my world, you would be celebrated. They would understand you and revere you. You could truly be a queen there, a great queen."

"Why?"

"You are strong, powerful, and brave. In my world, those traits are valued and admired."

"How would people in your world see that I am strong and powerful? They don't know me."

Charli sensed an opening and continued.

"In my world, there is a thing called money. It is valued above everything else. If you have a lot of it, you are automatically strong and powerful and admired."

"Money? What is that?"

Charli paused, collecting her thoughts. Even though she had gone over and over this in her mind countless times, she hadn't yet faced the challenge of describing money to someone who knew nothing about it. Money, an abstract concept that was so fundamental to her world was unknown to these people.

"Money is an idea of a person's worth based on the things they possess. Certain things are worth a great deal of money, so if you have a lot of those things, you are also worth a great deal."

"What are those things?"

Charli could sense that she was on a roll now. She didn't dare look over at Joslyn as it would have distracted her. She had rehearsed this next part of her argument many times, so that it was well-practiced.

"The ruby stones that the Q'ehazi use at the Honor Stone in my world would be worth a huge amount of money. That was why Sean wanted to take them back with him. He was planning to sell them so that he could be powerful and admired."

Barylos was putting two and two together.

"So, if I took back some ruby stones with me to your world, I would also be powerful and admired?"

"Yes!" Charli encouraged, getting a little carried away.

"You would be powerful and admired, much more than you'd ever be here. They'd probably make you Queen immediately."

Even though she knew this wasn't strictly the truth, she wanted to impress upon Barylos the benefits to her of following through on her proposed plan.

Barylos mused aloud for a few moments.

"So, instead of going to war against the Q'ehazi and taking back my rightful Queendom by force, I could journey to a place where I would be immediately crowned?" She mulled the idea over in her mind, and a slow smile spread over her face.

"Well, little Charlotte Grace, your idea certainly has some potential, but how do I get to your world? If it's so easy, why hasn't it been done before?"

This was the coup de grâce. "I know the way. I can lead you to the portal and show you how to cross over to the other world."

"Would I be able to return to Q'ehazi?"

"You won't want to, I'm sure," Charli replied quickly. She hadn't thought Barylos would ever want to come back, and she certainly didn't want to make a way for her to return.

Barylos fixed her with a steely glare, indicating that she had arrived at a decision.

"Very well. I will go with you through the portal and into your world. I will take my followers with me since they would not be welcome anymore in Q'ehazi. We will journey together to the Honor Stone, and take the ruby stones as you suggest. I will leave my homeland forever, believing that your world will be a better place for me, a place where I and my kind will be more accepted."

Charli's relief spread over her face, and she couldn't contain her joy.

"But!" Barylos put up a warning finger. "We will do a fair exchange. Tit for tat, as they say. An eye for an eye."

Charli frowned, wondering what Barylos was planning to suggest.

"If I have to leave my home forever, so should you. If I can never again return to Q'ehazi, you also can never again return to your home. Once you have led me through the portal, you will say goodbye to your world forever and remain in Q'ehazi. Do you agree to these terms?"

Charli paused, thinking about her mother who would miss her terribly and of her promising career as a psychologist that she'd worked so hard to create for herself. She glanced over at Joslyn, and his handsome face was impassive. She thought about all the experiences she'd had in Q'ehazi, and how she loved the people here and felt truly accepted here, so much more than in her own world where she had struggled to fit in.

"Yes," she replied.

"Then we have an agreement."

In common with the Villagers of the Far Northwest, Barylos and her army of Liberation Warriors rode horses from place to place. They planned to send an army of about 100 Liberation Warriors on horseback to make the 2,000-mile trek back to the Q'ehazi homeland. Navigating the narrow isthmus was no problem so long as they timed it correctly, and the snow-capped mountain had to be traversed around its low-lying base rather than going across the top since the horses had their limitations when climbing to a peak.

What would have taken Charli and Joslyn several weeks to walk around the base of the mountain was accomplished in a less than a month on horseback. Now they could traverse many more miles in one day than would have been possible on foot.

Barylos traveled in a wagon pulled by two of her most devoted followers on horseback. However, the army couldn't spare any of their best horses so Charli and Joslyn rode an old nag that was well past her prime. Charli and Joslyn sat on this horse and took turns guiding her with the reins. She was old and slow, and they frequently ambled along at the back of the group. Barylos exhorted them to "hurry up and keep up" but no amount of her yelling made the old horse go any faster. She was tired after a lifetime of carrying riders.

Then one day the inevitable happened. The horse lost her footing on a loose rock and stumbled, falling to her knees and collapsing, throwing Charli and Joslyn to the ground. The horse groaned in pain, as Joslyn sprang to his feet and examined her.

"She's broken her hind leg," he announced to the rest of the group. "She can't go on."

The wagon train stopped, and Barylos got out of her wagon to investigate what was going on. When she saw the horse on the ground with Joslyn bent over the animal, she immediately ascertained what had happened, "This horse is done. We'll have to shoot it." Then, noticing Charli's look of dismay at the bluntness of this command, she added, "To put it out of its misery."

"Please, wait," argued Joslyn, as one of the warriors aimed a rifle at the horse. "I understand that she can't continue, and she needs to be put down as humanely as possible, but can I just talk to her first?"

"Sure," sneered Barylos, returning to her wagon in disgust. "Just don't be too long about it. You two will have to walk the rest of the way. Fortunately, we've already done the majority of our journey, so I'm certain you can handle it."

Charli looked at Joslyn in wonderment, as she saw him bend over the horse and gently stroke its neck. It reminded her powerfully of the golden bear incident when Joslyn had performed a similar ritual.

"I'm sorry," she heard him murmur softly to the horse as it lay gasping for breath. "You can go peacefully now; no more labor for you."

A shot rang out, and the horse was no more.

Charli didn't cry, but she did feel tears pricking at her eyes, as the army of Liberation Warriors moved away from the horse on the ground. Apart from Joslyn's brief ceremony, nothing had been done to ritualize the animal's passing, and Charli could feel how this tore at Joslyn's heart.

The two of them walked on in silence until gradually night fell and the army made its camp for the night in their tents. Joslyn and Charli used their small tent that they had managed to save from the waters of the isthmus. They huddled in it for warmth against the cold night air. They kept mostly to themselves and didn't interact with the others any more than was absolutely necessary.

The next morning, Joslyn was the first to awaken and soon was aware of an unusual commotion outside. So, he gently jostled Charli and they both stumbled out of their tent to see what was going on. Two men were yelling at each other, and Barylos was standing with her hands on her hips appearing angry and frustrated.

"How the hell did it get away?" she demanded.

"We usually tie them up for the night. It must have been Igado. He's young and doesn't know how to tie the ropes properly," said Tyson, the older of the two disgruntled men. The young man stood back from the crowd with his head lowered in shame.

"So, it was you?" Barylos snapped.

"Yes," the youngster admitted, in a low mutter.

"Why wasn't he trained properly?" said Barylos to Tyson. "Don't you believe it's important that our horses stay with us, especially one of our best horses, the one pulling *my wagon?*"

"Yes, of course," Tyson replied, sheepishly.

Barylos grunted in disgust. "I'm going to get myself a cup of cacao juice now, but you better find that horse and bring it back. You'll have to figure it out between yourselves." She stomped off back to her wagon, leaving the others to glance around in bewilderment.

Joslyn, having overheard this conversation, went up to Tyson. "I believe I can find the lost horse," he stated.

"You? Why?" the man replied. Tyson was about 50 years old, with hair just graying at the temples and a broad, sun-weathered face.

"He has a way with horses," Charli chimed in, joining them in the discussion. "You should see him, he's amazing." She remembered how

Joslyn had tamed the horse for the young girl from the Village of the Far Northwest and how grateful the villagers had been. Charli was also hopeful that this might be a way to gain favor with Barylos and make their journey a little easier.

"I tell you what. If you can find the horse, I'll be so grateful. I'll let you both ride on my horse for the rest of the journey and I'll walk in your place."

"It is agreed," responded Joslyn, shaking Tyson's hand. "If you can let Charli and me borrow your horse for a few minutes, we can ride around the area and try to find the missing animal."

Tyson agreed rather reluctantly to this plan, realizing that there wouldn't be any need for the two strangers to ride away since they had suggested this journey in the first place. He also knew it would make their job of finding the lost animal much easier as they could quickly cover a wide area of land in search of the horse.

So, Charli and Joslyn set out on Tyson's horse to search for the missing beast. "Where do you think we should look first?" asked Charli to Joslyn in thought-words.

"I have a good idea where that horse might be," Joslyn responded in the same way. Sure enough, he confidently retraced their steps of the day before back to the place where their other horse had been shot. It took them about half an hour to reach the spot they had spent several hours traversing the day before because they were so much slower on foot.

When they reached the place, Charli saw the old nag on the ground with a few flies buzzing around her. To her amazement, she also saw the lost horse standing over its dead companion.

"You see? They were friends," reported Joslyn in thought-words, as he noticed Charli's astonishment. "I had noticed that fact about these two. So, I surmised the wagon-pulling horse would be wondering what had happened to his companion and might come looking for her."

"It's amazing," gasped Charli, her hand to her mouth. "I had no idea animals could form bonds like this."

"Oh, they are far more intelligent than we think." Joslyn alighted from the horse he had been sharing with Charli and gently but firmly led the other horse away and jumped on its back. "Let's go back and tell them the good news."

"They'll be so happy."

Joslyn smiled, "We will also be happy that we don't have to walk the rest of the way!"

Chapter Sixteen

The journey back to Central Q'ehazi where Sovereign Aurora lived took several weeks on horseback. Barylos and her entourage were unable to travel on the moving conveyor belt that was the main method of transportation in Q'ehazi because of their horses and wagons.

Barylos would have spurned the use of anything that smacked of Q'ehazi customs and culture, so determined was she to repudiate their way of life. As they arrived at the outskirts of Q'ehazi Land, there were times when journeying beside the conveyor belt was unavoidable, and Charli looked longingly at the happy and peaceful people sitting inside and wished that she was not part of this troupe of warriors.

Sometimes, the passengers' curious stares greeted them as their group of roughly 100 people traveling by horseback and wagon was an unusual sight and worthy of comment. Charli wished she could say something like "Don't count me as one of them. Look, I'm with Joslyn who is Aurora's son and one of you." She tried thinking this in thought-words to them, but perhaps the distance was too great or there were too many distractions, as nobody on the conveyor belt ever seemed to notice them.

Joslyn, on the other hand, was unperturbed or perhaps he was just lost in reflection that was not communicated because he stared straight ahead silently even in his thoughts. Charli felt consumed by swirling emotions that she longed to express, but Joslyn's stoical demeanor formed a wall between them and so she was silent but for different reasons.

Autumn was descending on the Earth at this time, and the nights were chilly. The travelers' tents provided them with little protection from the cold air. Even Barylos was not immune from this change in temperature, and Charli frequently heard her coughing at night, as the tents were all pitched close to each other. The meager provisions that Barylos' soldiers had prepared for the journey were not sufficient, and the soldiers had to start rationing food, and this contributed to the general malaise and feeling of ill-health that permeated their little encampment.

Joslyn had a tendency to get out of their makeshift bed first in the morning to perform his ablutions. Charli was not surprised to see that the space beside her was empty after she opened her eyes one morning and sleepily shivered in the morning air.

Suddenly, the tent flap opened, and Joslyn peered in. He spoke urgently and aloud. "Charli, get up. We need you." It was unusual for Joslyn to issue a command such as this, and Charli immediately recognized the tension in his voice, which caused her stomach to flutter. She dressed hurriedly and left the tent, then looked around to see what was happening.

She spotted a little group of people speaking in hushed yet forceful voices, and Joslyn, who was among them, waved at her to approach them. Charli hurried over and noticed that the group was standing outside Barylos' tent and Tyson was with them. Since he was one of the few people she somewhat knew, she gave him a brief smile of recognition. His expression was stern, and he didn't return her smile, which indicated to her that something was seriously wrong.

"Barylos is sick," he announced. "Joslyn tells us you may be able to help."

"Me?" Charli was stunned. "But I thought..."

"I am a doctor, yes," Joslyn interrupted her, knowing the end of her sentence, "but I don't have any of my herbs with me. Do you remember the pouch of herbs that you received from Juvana's mother that you used to heal me after the bear attack? Do you still have that pouch?"

Charli knew exactly what he meant, and she remembered where she kept the pouch. In fact, her usual routine was to put it around her neck as soon as she rose in the morning. However, this morning she had forgotten to do that during her rushed exit from the tent. Everyone seemed to be looking at her expectantly. She stood for a moment, feeling stupid with her mouth slightly agape.

"Do you have the pouch of herbs?" Joslyn repeated, a note of irritation in his voice.

Charli felt oddly betrayed at that moment. Was she really supposed to help the enemy? Barylos was Joslyn's sister, yes, but she had never behaved as such. She never lost an opportunity for deriding the Q'ehazi people, of which he was one. She had been mean to them and even threatened to have them killed! Charli looked at Joslyn, and she knew he understood what was going through her mind, even without thought-words. He pursed his lips and gave a slight nod and sent his thought-words, "I understand your hesitation, but now you need to do the right thing, even if it doesn't feel good."

Charli obediently went back to the tent, retrieved the pouch from its customary hiding place, and returned to the waiting group. She gave the pouch to Joslyn, but he gave it back to her.

"They are your herbs," he instructed, "Now it is up to you."

Again, Charli felt like a little girl who was being admonished, but she fought off the part of her that wanted to rebel and entered Barylos' tent, clutching the pouch of herbs.

Barylos was laying on a bed of cushions, and she was not dressed in her usual khaki uniform, but in loose-fitting clothes that were draped around her thin body. She seemed smaller, somehow. Charli had never realized how slight the older woman's figure was because usually the strength of her personality gave her the impression of being a large person, yet she was hardly taller than Charli. Barylos' face was very pale, her hair unkempt, and her voice weak as she whispered, "I feel terrible. Joslyn said you could help me."

In that moment, seeing her like that, Charli's compassion overcame her resentment, and her desire to help was genuine. "Yes, I have some herbs that were given to me by the people of the Far North Village. I was told they could cure just about anything."

"Thank you."

Charli was surprised by Barylos' expression of gratitude and her wan smile. With the aid of some of Barylos' warriors who were in the tent, Charli quickly made a poultice of some of the herbs and laid it on Barylos' chest. Even though she wasn't a doctor, she could tell by the constant coughing she had heard that the problem was stemming from that area and that a warm poultice might clear some of the phlegm from her lungs.

In a few hours, Barylos sent the message that she was well enough to travel, and the troupe was instructed to pack up their tents and continue the journey.

To Charli's surprise, this incident lowered the wall that she had felt between herself and Joslyn. He even smiled at her at times, pointed out the names of trees and birds that he knew, and was generally happier and more like the quiet yet easy-going person she had come to know before this journey. Perhaps, she contemplated, it was partly because they were getting closer and closer to the center of Q'ehazi Land and the end of their trip.

In fact, it was only a few days later that they became aware of the daily 3:00 p.m. rain shower that demonstrated they were really in Q'ehazi Land. The trees were becoming more plentiful, and Charli could sometimes spot a friendly deer or a small squirrel playing in the branches. It wouldn't be long now before they arrived at the Village of the Elders where Sovereign Aurora resided, which was their planned destination. Charli felt a little nervous at the thought that, even though this part of their journey was coming to a close, her responsibilities moving forward were beginning, and she hoped she could accomplish what she had set out to achieve.

Chapter Seventeen

Charli was seated beneath a canopy of leaves feeling more peaceful than she had ever felt in her life. Perhaps because of the dramatic events of the past few days and weeks and the turbulence of her emotions—fear, anger, and sadness—this calm state was a welcome contrast, and Charli reveled in it, taking in the sounds of intermittent bird songs, distant flute music as somebody rehearsed on one of the grassy knolls that punctuated the hillside, the sight of lazy clouds dotting a cerulean blue sky above her head, and the scent of magnolia blossoms as they wafted on the air.

With her senses heightened to experience all of these things, Charli was re-acquainted with her reasons for wanting to be in the world of the Q'ehazi and perhaps remain here forever. She hadn't considered the possibility of this latter option, having been too focused on re-entering through the portal and helping Abbe and Sovereign Aurora regain their status in their world. But the thought flitted across her mind that her ability to remain in Q'ehazi could be a direct result of her actions in successfully persuading Barylos to dispel her ideas of conquering Q'ehazi in favor of potential power and influence in another more suitable world.

Charli felt no qualms about giving up residence in her world. Despite her erstwhile dreams about becoming a licensed psychologist and helping others, she had a feeling she could do far better in this place where the people lived more in line with her values. She had promised Barylos and would keep her promise to live in Q'ehazi forever and forego any visits to her previous place or residence.

Just one thing plagued her and occupied her mind: her mother. Charli knew Angela would be upset at the thought of never seeing her daughter again. The two had become closer these past few years, and Charli had no desire to hurt or abandon her mother. It was her intention, therefore, to visit her mother after taking Barylos and the followers through the portal and try to persuade her mother to return with her to Q'ehazi so they could live there together. Surely, once Angela had been introduced to this wonderful world, she would love it as much as her daughter did, and she'd have no problem sacrificing the familiar pleasures of her world and leaving them behind.

Charli heard a rustling behind her, and Abbe appeared through the trees clutching a mug of a warm liquid. Abbe smiled and projected thought-words to her friend, "Hello, little sister. I've brought you a *Pukatl* drink that we use for comfort and reassurance. I know you've been through a lot, and you must be tired."

"Thank you," responded Charli, taking the drink gratefully and sipping the warm liquid. "Hmm, that's tastier than your other medicinal one."

"That's right. We like to spice it up a bit and make it more appetizing. There's some cinnamon and cloves and a pinch of ginger." Abbe always took great pleasure in explaining recipes, using her hands to show the tiny amounts she was indicating.

"I heard the violin. Have you been rehearsing?"

"Yes, we have a big concert coming up for the equinox celebration next week. Mother said you arrived back at the perfect time."

"Why is that?" Charli responded, warming her hands on the steaming mug.

"The people were starting to become worried. They didn't know if Barylos was planning to attack as she had threatened, and they certainly didn't know how to defend themselves. Aurora has been trying to reassure them that all is well, but you know we didn't hear from you for a long time."

"I know. I was trying and trying to send thought messages to you, but it didn't seem to work."

"I understand. Sometimes, when a person is under extreme stress or facing a crisis, their psychic powers become diminished, and they can no longer communicate in that way."

"Maybe that's why none of Barylos' followers use the thought-words," mused Charli.

"That's right! They speak only aloud."

"Yes, and usually loudly!"

"It's so strange how they've made themselves so different from us, and from the place they are from. They refuse to take the *Pukatl*; they no longer use thought-words; they have no wish to attain a *State of Grace*; and they have weapons." Abbe made a gesture with her hands, indicating that she didn't know if there were other things she might not know about.

"When I told them about money, they were very interested. Seems like they are almost exactly like the people in my world and not like Q'ehazi people at all."

"So that is how you managed to persuade them?"

"Yes. When I told Barylos that she could be powerful—and rich— she really liked that idea, and she decided it was better to join my world than to try and take over Q'ehazi."

"What do you mean by rich?"

Charli gave a brief sigh, reflecting on how odd this question would seem back in her world. "Rich means having a lot of money."

"And having a lot of money means what?"

"Having a lot of power and telling other people what to do."

"Barylos would like that for sure," mused Abbe. "She used to boss Joslyn and me around when we were kids. She said it was because she was the older one. Joslyn is older than me, but he was never bossy like that."

Charli smiled at this mention of her friend and enjoyed the visualization of him as a child. "I bet he was always gentle like he is now."

"Oh yes, he was. I was surprised that he offered to go with you as he's not usually brave in that way. Maybe it's because he likes you." Abbe had a little quizzical expression that Charli found difficult to interpret, but she decided not to pursue this topic of conversation.

"Where is he?"

"He went back to the Village of Healers to see his friends. He will join us for dinner tonight. Aurora has asked the others to prepare a feast for us in honor of your successful journey."

"That sounds good." The food was always so delicious in Q'ehazi and so freshly prepared that she could only imagine what a feast would entail. She anticipated that it would be wonderful. Then a thought occurred to her and she asked, "Barylos isn't coming, is she?"

"Oh no, of course not," reassured Abbe. "They are all staying in an unpopulated area nearby. Sovereign Aurora made it clear that she didn't want them interacting with the Q'ehazi people and possibly influencing them to join her. She's done enough damage. Tomorrow you will all meet at the place of the Honor Stone and give Barylos her ruby stones before you lead her and her followers through the portal into the other world."

Charli paused for a moment, wondering whether she should share her ideas with her friend. Fortunately, Abbe's attention was diverted by a deer grazing nearby. Abbe pointed the deer out to Charli. The moment for any revelations passed, so Charli contented herself by making a vague comment, "I hope I can make the right decisions."

"You must do whatever you believe in your heart is right," concluded Abbe. "My mother believes you have attained a *State of Grace* that will lead you in the right direction, so long as you listen carefully to your inner voice and follow its promptings."

Later that night, when dinner and all the celebrations were over, Charli and Joslyn met in a clearing in the forest to say goodnight. The first thing Joslyn did when he saw Charli was to approach her and give her a long, warm hug. As Charli surrendered to his tender embrace, she smelled the notes of cinnamon and jasmine on his jacket and felt his scratchy beard touch her chin, and she thought of how much she loved this man and everything about him.

After he pulled away, he gazed at her directly and intently for a few moments without speaking either in thoughts or words. She also looked into his big, warm, brown eyes and knew that communication could be without thoughts or words just pure feelings as if they were creatures meeting in the forest for a silent bonding.

"Taking that journey with you has helped me know you," Joslyn finally said in thought-words. "My mother says you have attained a *State of Grace* and I agree. You are an incredible person. An incredible woman," he added, with a small smile.

Charli felt overwhelmed with love and gratitude (mingled with a little inner guilt about the secret plan she was harboring), and she didn't know how to respond.

"You are incredible, too," she blurted out in a girlish display of awkwardness and enthusiasm, trying to subtly shift the conversation to a less intimate topic, when she wasn't really at all sure she really had attained the *State of Grace* that Joslyn referred to. She wanted to ask, *What actually is a State of Grace and how did I attain it? I mean, I wasn't trying to get it as I was just doing my best.* She realized that this thought was transmitted instantly to Joslyn, and he responded.

"Everyone struggles with the *State of Grace*. Yes, even me."

"You?" Charli was shocked.

Joslyn's responding smile was mysterious. "Perhaps you think I'm perfect and, of course, I enjoy seeming that way to you. But I can assure you that I am not. There was a time when I….." He lowered his head in reflection as if trying to find the words to express his meaning. Serai's face flashed upon his consciousness as a pang of guilt swept through him. "I hurt someone very deeply. I didn't mean to."

Charli grabbed his hand impulsively and squeezed it, her eyes expressing earnest encouragement. Her thought-words were, "You are a good person, Joslyn. We all make mistakes."

Joslyn chuckled and briefly kissed the hand that squeezed his. "You see, you are older than your years. Many people go straight to judgment and condemnation, but you always seek to understand."

Charli's corresponding frown demonstrated confusion. Joslyn continued in thought-words.

"The *State of Grace* is somewhat indefinable, but as my mother puts it, it's a combination of courage, integrity, compassion. and empathy. You displayed empathy when you helped Sean get back to his world even at a cost to you. You displayed great courage in volunteering to travel to the home of Barylos despite the dangers involved. You displayed compassion when you healed my wounds after the bear attack, and when you healed Barylos from her sickness. I believe that integrity is part of who you are." Joslyn smiled at his last statement.

Charli was at a loss for how to respond, so she remained silent and uncharacteristically tongue-tied with a vague dreamy smile on her face.

"There was a reason you came back here. I believe there is a reason for every action that a person takes, a reason for everything that happens. Yes, you wanted to help the Q'ehazi people, but there was also another reason."

Charli nodded and admitted with a wry smile, "I wanted to see you again."

"We never spoke of these things on our journey because it was too fraught with danger and the unexpected. But now that the journey is over, or almost over, this is a time for softness and reconnection." Joslyn's face was serious but not somber. He spoke directly with no artifice or pretension, and that was unfamiliar to Charli, but it also gave her permission to be similarly honest and direct.

"Can I ask you what are your feelings for me?"

Charli replied, "I wanted to see you again because I knew when I first met you that we had a special connection all those years ago. I wondered and hoped you were not already married to some nice Q'ehazi girl."

Joslyn's mouth twitched upwards in a smile. "Many girls here are nice, yes, but I wasn't ready."

"I was so glad to hear you were not. I have had some connections with other people in my world, but nothing ever felt so real and true as what I felt with you. During the journey, our connection only grew stronger."

"You are right." Joslyn took Charli's hand in his and led her through the trees. "Here in Q'ehazi, we enjoy our rituals and our ceremonies. The first thing two people do when they feel a connection such as we feel, is they sleep together in the same hammock. Would you do me the honor of sleeping in my hammock with me tonight?"

Charli felt her heart lift inside her chest almost to her throat. She could hardly contain her excitement and joy. "Yes!" was her one-word answer that did not at all sum up her emotions at that moment.

Charli had been accused at earlier times of being too much "in her head" and too focused on analyzing experiences rather than just living or enjoying them. But in this instance, she allowed pure sensation to overcome her, turning off her over-active mind and just responding as a child or an animal who is completely in the present moment.

Joslyn was gentle and he was also a man, and she realized at once that he was experienced and confident in the art of love-making.

Excitement mingled with desire, as he led her by the hand and took her to his hammock. These were sensations she had never felt with Nick who seemed like a mere boy in comparison.

Later she would recall the scent of his warm brown body, the sweetness of his tender touch as he stroked her, and the strength of his embrace as she twined her legs around his back and arched her body to meet his. When he entered her, it felt as though she was now complete, that a part of her had been missing all these years and was now found, and she never wanted him to leave.

The sounds of their love-making mingled with the animal and insect noises of the night around them, so that everything felt so natural and so a part of the organic natural world. There was no distinction between them and the trees where the hammock was slung or the ground over which they lay. Charli finally had the completely visceral sense of "We Are All One" that she had only intuited before, but now that phrase made sense to her, and she knew what it meant.

"We Are All One," the voice inside her head said, "Me, Joslyn, the trees, the hammock, the earth, the animals, the ruby stones, We Are All One, and we are beautiful."

Chapter Eighteen

Charli felt differently the next day at a small ceremony at the Honor Stone held by Sovereign Aurora to hand over some ruby stones to Barylos. As Charli watched, Barylos received five of the precious ruby stones and placed them in a woven wicker basket. Charli felt a sense of possessiveness she hadn't noticed before, a feeling that these valuable gems should not be given away, especially to somebody like Barylos who cared nothing for Q'ehazi and its people but lusted only for her own power and influence. Then, of course, Charli remembered this whole affair had been her idea, and there was a good purpose behind it that would save the Q'ehazi people from any harm or attacks by Barylos and her followers.

The Liberation Warriors had not been invited to the ceremony, and neither had anybody else from Q'ehazi because Sovereign Aurora wanted to avoid any chaos or confusion. Not everybody needed to understand the reasons behind the ceremony that day, and it was deemed best that they should remain uninformed about this transaction.

For her part, Sovereign Aurora acted with her customary grace and dignity, as she handed over each stone to her daughter and reminded her of their intrinsic value and worth. Barylos was strangely humbled by this exchange, her usual bravado silenced, as she accepted these gifts and promised to take care of them as befitted these stones' value and beauty. Charli, watching, didn't know how likely Barylos would fulfill this promise once she knew the rubies could be exchanged for money in her world. That was far more valuable to *her* because it represented the power and the influence she craved so exclusively. The stones were each wrapped abundantly in cloth, so they would be protected from the toxic air of the other universe until they could be kept safely in a location indoors.

Once the ceremony was over, Barylos retreated to the long building where her army waited for her. She watched as her followers gathered up their possessions in preparation for the journey ahead. Each of Barylos' soldiers was equipped with a knapsack containing a gun and a few provisions, and each wore a uniform of khaki pants and a jacket. Charli accompanied Barylos to her soldiers' temporary encampment. They looked incongruous in the lush green forests of Q'ehazi that had never seen weapons, soldiery, or uniforms, and Charli sensed that they were anticipating joining another world that would fit them much better.

Before she returned to her village, Sovereign Aurora gave Charli a strong hug and a kiss on both cheeks with a fond farewell, saying in thought-words, "You are brave, dear sister, I wish you Godspeed on your journey and return to us soon." Aurora had started calling Charli "sister" as a token of respect and familial ties that went beyond mere biology. "I am glad you decided to choose Q'ehazi as your permanent home. You know you are always welcome to stay here."

"Yes, I'll be glad to come home again," replied Charli, noting how easily the word "home" slipped out as she thought of Q'ehazi in that regard now. "I want to try and bring my mother here as I don't like the idea of abandoning her."

"She is welcome here, but it is her choice, of course."

Charli hadn't considered the possibility that her mother might not wish to come back to Q'ehazi with her, as to her, the world of Q'ehazi was in every way preferable to the other world she knew. She pushed away the idea that her mother might not want to accompany her, and she concluded her powers of persuasion would have the effect she wished.

Pushing through the trees at around midday, at the head of a long line of Liberation Warriors, Charli was reminded about the first time she discovered this world and all the adventures she had encountered. As it was only a couple of miles from the Honor Stone location to the portal at the Redbud Tree, Barylos and her followers abandoned their vehicles and horses and walked this part of the journey. Charli walked in front flanked by two of Barylos' soldiers— one male, one female— who walked on either side of her and almost touching her as if they were afraid she might run away and abandon this mission. Barylos sat in a make-shift rickshaw that was carried by four of her soldiers, giving her the impression of a queen or empress who was too grand to set foot on humble ground. Nobody spoke or communicated, and their journey to the tree was a silent one.

Charli felt some trepidation about what she was about to experience. She had promised to take Barylos and her followers back to her own world and to leave them there. Barylos had been quite insistent that Charli had to forfeit any right she may have to live in her own world from now on, and that she should immediately retrace her steps and never return. Charli was happy with her choice to remain in Q'ehazi as an alternative to living in her own world. But two things were still bothering her, and they were uppermost in her mind as she approached the portal.

She had considered tricking Barylos and her followers by taking them not into her own world, but into that Hellscape World that she had encountered for a short while when searching for Q'ehazi. She wondered if it was quite honest and ethical to do that, which was not officially what she had promised. Was she, in fact, justified in leaving Barylos in a world that was so heinous, even though Barylos had proven herself to be not a fit candidate for Q'ehazi and certainly lacking a *State of Grace*? Wouldn't her own world suffer by having someone such as

Barylos added to it, especially with her followers and their weapons, and the ruby stones giving them money and power?

Charli thought mostly of her mother and how she didn't want the gentle Angela to be at the mercy of anyone such as Barylos. Even though Charli's mother had met and settled down with a nice man who treated her well, she still had a certain innocence about her and an inability to navigate the worst excesses of this complex world. Plus, there were many other women like Angela, who would fall prey to a person like Barylos when given money and the power to behave in whatever manner she pleased.

Charli wanted to protect her mother. This led to her second qualm. She had promised Barylos that immediately upon entering her world through the portal and successfully taking the leader and her supporters there, Charli would go back to Q'ehazi and forego any connection with her own world. She was happy to do that, but she was intensely anxious to contact her mother and ask her to return with her to Q'ehazi. Even if Angela didn't want to come with her, Charli wanted to be able to see her mother maybe if only to say goodbye for the last time and tell her where she was going.

Charli couldn't bear the thought of vanishing one day with Angela having no idea what had happened to her daughter. She knew that would be devastating to her mother, and she didn't want to cause her such pain. But how could she explain this to Barylos who was not exactly the most empathetic of people at the best of times and who would potentially jeer at her sensitivities? Still, Barylos also had a mother and couldn't be completely without human understanding.

The sun was high in the sky, and everyone was hot and sweaty by the time they reached the Redbud Tree. Charli indicated to her soldier consorts that they had reached their destination. Barylos descended from her rickshaw and instructed all of her followers to don their masks in preparation for traveling to the other world and dealing with the toxic air there. "So, where is this magical portal?" Barylos asked, approaching Charli with a skeptical air. "I don't see anything different here."

"It's the tree," Charli replied, pointing to the trunk of the Redbud Tree.

"That?" Barylos scoffed, with a brief chuckle. "I had imagined something a little more imposing."

"Well, if it looked special, I guess everyone would be going through it, wouldn't they?" offered Charli. She was surprised to notice Barylos had no rejoinder for that comment, and this gave Charli a little confidence.

"I'll be the first to go through, and then you should follow me, one by one," Charli instructed in a voice loud enough for Barylos and all her followers to hear. "The portal will remain open only for about 40 minutes, so we need to hurry."

The soldiers seemed uncertain of how to proceed, so Barylos urged them to comply. "You heard her!" she ordered. "Get into single file behind the girl. I will be the last person through."

Charli was unsure whether Barylos was demonstrating courage by allowing her followers to go through first or if she wanted to be sure there was no danger in this action before taking it herself. In any case, as soon as her orders were given, the soldiers formed an orderly line behind Charli and waited for the portal to open.

Charli put her hand on the trunk of the tree and felt the slight dizzy sensation and the blurring of her eyes that she knew well. She opened the tear as wide as she could to allow the others to follow and stepped forward. In a few minutes, all of the soldiers were standing beside the well-known creek in Charli's world and Barylos brought up the rear.

The woman looked around her with a quizzical air. "So, this is your home, is it? It doesn't look much different."

"That's right, it doesn't seem to be much different at first glance," Charli agreed. "But look off in the distance. Do you see those buildings? There are many houses here, unlike in Q'ehazi." Barylos and her followers dutifully inspected the distant landscape and a few murmurs proved that they had seen the buildings and realized they were in a different world.

"Also, if you look up at the sky, you may see some white streaks from the contrails. You don't have that in Q'ehazi."

"Ah, yes, it's true!" exclaimed one man looking upwards. "I've never seen anything like those lines in the sky. What are contrails?"

But Barylos cut him off with a wave of her hand. "And so, now, it is time for you to return to Q'ehazi and leave us here," reminded Barylos. "You need to go back before the portal closes again."

Charli spoke quickly, knowing she would have to get this over with before her courage faded. "Yes, I want to go back and I *will* go back, but I just have one small errand first."

"What?" snapped Barylos, looking genuinely shocked. "You never said anything about this errand before."

"I know, and I'm sorry, I really am. But it's important. It's my mother. I need to say goodbye to her first."

"You should have thought of that before you made your promise," Barylos warned, in a cold voice.

"I'm not reneging on my promise, not at all," pleaded Charli. "I just want my mom to know where I am so she doesn't worry about me. I'm her only child."

"There's no time for that," said Barylos with an air of finality. The soldiers around her were also getting impatient and some murmurs were rustling among them.

"She's just over there so if I run, I can be there in five minutes. It won't take me long. Please. She'll be so upset if I disappear and she never knows what happened to me. Please. It doesn't matter to you. It's this one little thing."

"It *does* matter to me; it matters a lot that you've been lying to us all this time."

"No, no! I wasn't lying, I swear I wasn't. I *want* to be in Q'ehazi forever, I *do*. Why do you think I went back there in the first place?" Charli heard her voice pitch becoming higher as her anxiety tightened her throat to the verge of panic.

"You think I should trust you?" Barylos thundered. "You'll run off and disappear and we'll never see you again. You're deceitful! You tried to trick us!"

"No, no, I'm *not* lying. I'll run back as fast as I can. Please! We're wasting time as it is. You could send somebody with me, if you like, to make sure I don't disappear." Charli wondered if she'd come up with a good solution, and offered this to Barylos, her hands out in a pleading gesture and praying that the woman would soften and see her point of view.

But Barylos remained firm, and Charli started to recognize she was not a person who could be persuaded easily, especially once her mind was made up. Maybe that was why she had clashed so forcefully with her mother. In any case, this was no help to Charli. With hindsight, she wished she had organized a better plan or not left it until the last minute. Her denial and procrastination over the situation with her mother had landed her in this position, and now she had to wriggle her way out of the situation somehow.

Barylos' voice became louder and more insistent, as she continued to berate Charli, calling her a whore, a cheat, and a lying bitch. With this onslaught of hostility (maybe related only partly to current events and partly to Barylos' long-time resentment of the girl she still considered an intruder), Charli felt powerless to defend herself, and she stood frozen, speechless, and dumb with the shock of it all. Despite her consternation, some rational part of Charli's mind also managed to notice in an objective way that Barylos' face was becoming redder and more flushed with her rage, and this reminded Charli powerfully of those times when Sean had expressed similar unbridled hostility toward her mother, usually just before he became physically violent. Charli was afraid of Barylos at that moment, and she was terrified of the power the older woman wielded over her weapon-carrying soldiers. Charli's legs started to tremble like reeds in the wind, even as she stood her ground and maintained eye contact with the rageful woman confronting her.

Some of the Liberation Warriors were aware of their leader's anger, and perhaps in an effort to show support and devotion to her, they took up her insults and began to hurl them at Charli in a sort of chant, "She's a whore and a bitch, she's a whore and a bitch," over and over, while grinning and menacing Charli with their guns. Charli had never been more petrified, but she still stood and faced her accusers and her would-be attackers.

To Charli's horror, Barylos started ordering some of her soldiers to take out an ax from their backpack and chop down the Redbud Tree.

"You either go back to Q'ehazi now or you never go back," Barylos demanded. "It is your choice. If you don't go back to Q'ehazi now, we will destroy the portal and then you will have to stay here forever."

"What? No! What are you doing?" Charli felt faint and breathless with terror and panic. She felt like a cornered animal unable to go backwards or forwards. Lose Q'ehazi forever, or betray and abandon her mother? It was a horribly incomprehensible choice.

A wave of intense anxiety suddenly overwhelmed Charli. She started breathing rapidly from her chest, her palms felt sweaty, her heart was racing, and her stomach was in knots. Rapid thoughts occupied her mind, clouding her ability to think clearly. "What do I do? What do I do?" she repeated aloud. She closed her eyes momentarily and began rocking back and forth to calm herself. Then a miracle occurred.

The intensity of Charli's fear was literally bending her double. As she stretched to rise up again, she noticed the hazy blue line denoting the devastating and aptly named Hellscape World had again manifested itself in the middle of the creek. Her anxiety was instantly transformed to excitement, and she ran to the creek and sloshed through it, not even feeling the icy cold water. "It's here! It's here!" she screamed, pointing at the line. "This is the other world. This is it!"

One of Barylos' soldiers who had wandered off from the others and stood by the creek noticed Charli's agitated waving. He called out to his friends and to Barylos, "Hey, everybody, come quickly. There is a line here, a blue line. Look at this as it's really cool."

The others started to drift toward him, and Barylos' attention was sufficiently distracted that, to Charli's great relief, she shouted to her soldiers, "Leave that! We need you all over here now!" The men abandoned their efforts to cut down the Redbud Tree, while Barylos withdrew and crossed over to her soldiers to see what was happening.

Charli observed that Barylos was not happy with her undisciplined troops. Barylos even appeared a little flustered as she commanded them, "Nobody is to do anything without my authority!" Charli was aware that here was a person who needed to be in control and who was used to being obeyed in all things and to expecting her authority to be unquestioned. The idea of someone making a decision without her explicit instructions or discovering something unknown to her was a subtle undermining of her authority that ate away at her sense of absolute power over her subjects.

In that moment, Charli recognized the seeds of Barylos' downfall. Her tragic flaws were her inability to act in concert or collaboration with others and her need to micro-manage and control every situation in order to reassure her ego that her authority was not being thwarted. The woman's need for power had made her a leader in the first place, but it also made her a far less effective ruler than her mother who governed through mutual respect and trust rather than through fear and intimidation.

Charli was immensely grateful for this sudden and unexpected distraction. Barylos turned and followed some of her Liberation Warriors to the creek where a few of them were pointing and murmuring about their discovery. Charli tentatively followed but remained as far away as she could while still seeing what was going on.

Charli realized when she closed in on the spectacle that what the soldier discovered was the portal to the other world, the Hellscape World she had escaped from before finding Q'ehazi. The soldier who had made the discovery had actually stepped through the blue tear and into the other world, and some of the others were starting to follow him, curious as to what this other portal might be like.

Charli also realized that the intense emotions of anger and hostility that had been provoked in Barylos by Charli's refusal to immediately comply with her wishes led directly to the opening of this portal. In the same way as the portal to Q'ehazi was opened by a beloved object or part of that world (such as the shawl, the ruby stones, and the *Putkatl* fruit), the portal to *this world* was opened by a strong negative emotion, such as intense fear, anger, or sadness. Sean had been drawn into this world by his unfair acquisition of the ruby stone and his anger toward Charli. In her situation, Charli had been drawn in by her anger and fear and next Barylos and her supporters would be drawn into this world by their own wrath, chaos, and confusion.

Did this validate Charli's reasons for letting them enter what she knew to be a horrific and disturbing world? Did it take away any responsibility she had to save them from themselves, even if she could? She wasn't sure. But she did know that a person makes his or her own path in life, and this was the path that Barylos had chosen and that she was following, for good or ill, for herself and for her supporters.

Barylos walked to the edge of the blue tear leading to the other world. Even though some of the others had already entered this world of their own accord, Barylos insisted that the rest of her troops wait until she had passed through and given the order for them to follow. Accordingly, the warriors fell back and allowed their leader to pass through the tear.

Charli maintained her distance from the blue line hovering over the creek as she could see beyond and into the other world that wasn't at all like the world she had visited. A myriad of swirling colors and entrancing music invited people to enter. If Charli hadn't visited that world and didn't know what horrors lay beyond, she might have been seduced into stepping through that tear. But she had more knowledge than the others and kept this knowledge to herself.

One by one, the soldiers followed their leader into the other world—the Hellscape World—even though to them it was not how it appeared.

Charli felt enormous gratitude and relief that they left her alone in her world. She didn't even have to lure them into the other place because they went of their own accord.

"Come in, come in," came the siren call from the other Liberation Warriors who had gone to the other side. "It's beautiful here."

Charli didn't know why their experience of the other world was seemingly so different from what hers had been, but she had an intuition they would encounter something different in a little while, and she was ecstatic that she would not be a part of it.

As soon as the last person had gone through, Charli plunged into the icy waters of the creek, stepped up to the blue line, and with both hands firmly pushed the tear together, closing up the portal. Once it was closed, to her amazement and delight, the blue line completely disappeared.

She had just a few minutes to find her mother and persuade her to come back with her. Charli ran as fast as she could until she was gasping for breath. She arrived at her house and ran up the stairs, feeling intensely thankful when she noticed her mother's car was in the garage. That meant she was home from work.

When she reflected on it later, Charli's memory of that moment was a blur. She couldn't quite believe how she'd guided Barylos and her followers into their new world. Then there were all the other things she'd done: argued about seeing her mother, watched as all the soldiers disappeared unknowingly into the Hellscape World and it closed up forever; dashed back to her house and tried to persuade her mother to accompany her to Q'ehazi, returned to the Redbud Tree and passed through the portal in time before it closed up again—all in 40 minutes. She was young and her legs were strong, but she had never sprinted so fast in her life and probably never would again.

Charli was mortified that her mother had refused to come with her. If she was truly honest with herself, she also felt hurt and rejected. She'd been abandoned by her mother and there was no going back. She felt disappointed, confused, and painfully wounded. She was the only daughter her mother had. Didn't her mother *want* to share in her joy? Wasn't she *happy* that Charli had finally confided in her something so significant? Had Angela become so disconnected from Charli over these past few years while Charli was away in college that she no longer *cared* about the potential loss of her daughter forever? These questions—in fact, accusations—rumbled around in Charli's mind before she could stop them, and they pricked at her insides like insidious daggers.

Yet there was another way also to view the situation. Charli felt tremendous guilt at having not made any effort to tell her mother about Q'ehazi and share this extraordinary experience with her. This might have prepared Angela more persuasively and laid the groundwork for her to accompany her daughter.

When Charli assessed things more rationally, she saw that it must have been a huge shock to Angela to have her daughter burst through the door on a Wednesday afternoon and announce she only had a few minutes before she had to go to another world *forever*. She could never return home, and the only chance Angela had of being with her was to accompany her right then and there. Perhaps, it was just too much for the mother to bear.

Angela had become a lot more independent since Bill entered her life, and her self-esteem had grown, as Charli could see. Angela had her own life, and she was happy where she was. She had a job she enjoyed and a man who was emotionally supportive. Charli recognized she was no longer the center of her mother's world. It felt like a loss and yet strangely liberating at the same time. They would go their separate ways partly because of choices and partly because of the vagaries of circumstances. In the end, they would both be happy.

Charli ran to the Redbud Tree while praying that the tear would remain open long enough for her to return to her beloved Q'ehazi. As the brown line faded, she knew she only had seconds before it closed forever and she'd never go back because she no longer had the ruby stone left by Abbe to help her or any other way of returning.

She squeezed through the tear. Once on the other side of the Redbud Tree, Charli rested for the first time in hours and reflected that she was truly home at last and could stay forever.

Chapter Nineteen

It happened in a circle of oak and birch trees adorned with festive flowers, while musicians played. The Q'ehazi tradition was to have the ceremony in the village of the bride. Since Charli didn't officially belong to any village, her wedding was held at the Village of the Elders. Because the festivities were for Joslyn, the son of Sovereign Aurora, they were attended by people from far and wide as an important and special event. News spread quickly of Joslyn's marriage to the "girl from the Other World" as Charli was known, and everybody wished to attend and see this joyous occasion.

A feast was prepared by people from the Village of the Cooks, and Charli's dress was made by a friend of Abbe's from the Village of the Dressmakers. The dress was simple and comfortable to wear, and Charli was encouraged to keep wearing it after her wedding day and not put it away in a box as she would have done in her world. The Q'ehazi tradition did not require someone to give away the bride, such as her father, because she was not considered to be "owned" by anybody else but herself. It was normal for the man to join the family of the bride after the marriage, but since Charli was from far away, this situation was not normal and therefore she joined his family instead and they would continue to live in the Village of the Healers.

No rings were exchanged to symbolize fidelity. Instead, the couple was encouraged to create and provide love tokens of their choosing and give them to each other.

Some men and women from the Village of the Dancers had choreographed a beautiful dance that was enacted, as the musicians, including Abbe, played a piece of music that they composed especially for the occasion. In addition to the people who attended the ceremony, many different varieties of birds and animals came to pay their respects. Since the ceremony was conducted outdoors in an area generally frequented by animals who roamed freely about the neighborhood, many of them wandered about among the people. The birds in Q'ehazi were very tame and unafraid of people's interference and added their songs to the music.

When Charli was told that she was expected to create and bring a love token to the wedding, she was rather nonplussed and wondered what she could possibly offer that would be acceptable. She wondered if she could rise to this momentous occasion with a suitable gift for her betrothed, and it bothered her so much she asked Abbe for her help.

"As long as it comes from your heart, it will be the right gift," counseled Abbe to her friend, and so Charli thought long and hard and spent time outside in quiet reflection in order to prepare herself.

In her world, things were much more circumspect and as long as one followed the rules, it was relatively easy to do the right thing. Nobody was expected to create things from scratch or to really think for themselves. But here, that sort of creativity was very much encouraged, and while Charli celebrated this way of doing things, she also felt a little overwhelmed by the responsibility.

Since Joslyn was already a healer and that was also Charli's chosen profession in this world, she guessed her gift should be something connected to healing in some way. She also wanted something that represented her world.

When she created her gift, she enjoyed the process. When handing it to Joslyn at the ceremony, there was a little trepidation as she anticipated his response. The genuine pleasure on his face was sufficient reassurance that her gift was well-received: a wreath made out of branches of the Redbud Tree, twined together to form a circle. Charli didn't need to explain the significance of this to Joslyn, as she could see he understood at once that the Redbud Tree was the portal to her world, and the circle symbolized eternity.

Joslyn's gift to her made her eyes sparkle, and she trembled with emotion, as it was the most beautiful thing she'd ever seen. He took a ruby stone still adorning the Honor Stone location and carved it into a heart shape and then placed it on a chain so she could wear it around her neck. He lovingly placed it around her neck as the crowd looked on admiringly, and the two gazed into each other's eyes. No words were needed at this ceremony and none were spoken.

When the musicians and the dancers paused in their performances, Sovereign Aurora came and joined the lovers' hands together while saying aloud, "You are now joined as one, each equal and whole and yet a part of the other, and a part of the whole universe." Then everybody started singing the Welcome Song, and Joslyn and Charli joined in the songs and the dancing—the happiest moments of Charli's life.

Young Eliayo was one of the men tasked with cutting down the Redbud Tree that day. He was a young man, strong and healthy, and he enjoyed his apprenticeship as a carpenter. He wore his long, straight, silky black hair in a braid down his back, and it was often admired by onlookers, especially females, as it was his pride and joy.

It was a glorious summer day, full of bird songs and beauty, and the young man wished that this particular job had not been assigned to him, but he also understood the reason. It was not that it was a physically hard or difficult job, and he was usually very compliant with tasks assigned to him, especially when they came directly from the Sovereign.

He had been taught to value all living things, and especially trees, which were regarded as the life-blood of the planet and therefore sacred. He knew how trees communicated and, in common with his Q'ehazi brethren, he regularly talked to them and gave them names as part of their family. So, it went against the grain to be destroying this tree that was in its prime, just as he was about to do. Yet Sovereign Aurora had given the instruction to him and his two fellow woodworkers to chop down this particular tree thereby destroying the portal into the other world, so nobody else could come through it and invade the Q'ehazi world.

Eliayo and his two brethren laid their hands on the trunk of the tree and briefly said a prayer of thanks for the tree, as was their custom when killing any living thing for the benefit of their human society. Eliayo felt almost a visceral empathetic pain as the ax cut into the bark of the trunk for the first strike, and then fell again and again on the tree until it bent and finally crashed to the ground. It was not a very large or tall tree, and so it didn't take very long for the men to complete their work.

Once it was done, his two friends departed and went about their business, and Eliayo was supposed to place the now dead trunk and branches on to the communal firepit for burning later that week. But something stopped him from doing that task.

Eliayo was an artist and loved more than anything to create artifacts out of wood. He took the trunk back to his workshop located in a forest clearing close to the Village of the Woodworkers, and chopped the trunk into pieces after having carefully shaven off the branches and collecting them into a pile of firewood. The pieces of trunk were placed in a safe location away from the daily rains until he could get to carving. His intention was to create something special and unique from the trunk of this tree.

Eliayo was well aware of Charli's story as a visitor from another world, and he was grateful she had come to Q'ehazi and had managed to save them from Barylos and her army. At the same time, he recognized the need to close the portal to stop anybody else from entering into Q'ehazi who might be less benign. Thus, his intention was to create something that would honor Charli and her world from the tree that had let her enter into their world.

Over the next week or so, Eliayo spent all his free hours carving the pieces of wood. What he created was a beautiful wooden totem pole with carved representations of the plants and animals that surrounded him in the Q'ehazi world, such as flowers, squirrels, rabbits, and bees. When the carving was finished, he stained the timber with a dark resin that enhanced the color of the wood. Then he stepped back and surveyed his work. He was satisfied with the results. Each log that had been cut from the original tree had an image that faced in a different direction, which gave the totem pole an unusual three-dimensional quality.

He took the beautiful totem pole and placed it back in the spot where the original Redbud Tree had stood down by the creek. The darkly stained wood glinted in the sunlight, and Eliayo was happy. It was no longer a portal to another world. It was now a symbol of the connections between the two worlds and a celebration of the good things it had brought to both of them.

Chapter Twenty

Angela was crying often these days. She was annoying herself, and she knew that the very patient Bill was losing his patience with her constant mournfulness, and yet she was unable to stop crying. She had lost so much. Was there any hope for her after Charli left forever? Angela's sadness was exacerbated by her guilt over not choosing to go with her daughter when Charli had begged her to accompany her to the Redbud Tree and through the portal. Angela reflected so often upon that moment that it was burned into her memory in the same way a traumatic event imprints upon the brain as a constant and haunting reminder.

The prospect of a baby on the way comforted her but did little to assuage her guilt and responsibility about the way she handled her relationship with her first-born child.

Angela argued constantly with the little voice inside her head that said, "You should have gone with her, you idiot." She justified her inaction by reiterating that it had all happened so suddenly and with no forewarning. Was she supposed to make that tremendous decision to change her whole life right then with no preparation and not knowing about the consequences? She had never been a person to jump willingly into the unknown anyway, unlike Charli who was relatively impulsive and confident in her decisions. Angela had always preferred to not take risks and to comply with tradition as she had been taught. She was the opposite of a free thinker. She was the last person to make such a huge transition in her life, even when encouraged to do so by her daughter.

"I just couldn't think straight right then," Angela repeated to herself often when trying to validate her actions or rather her lack of action on that fateful day.

"I'm not a decisive person. There was no time anyway. I wish she would have given me more time to think about it. I'm pregnant, just turned 40, and might have complications from this second baby, plus who knows what the medical facilities are like in this other world?" Over and over, she came back to the same conclusions as her arguments circled back to the same results. No matter what justifications Angela had for her inaction, Charli was gone forever.

She knew Bill wanted her to get over it and to get on with her life. He had no idea what it was like to lose a child in such circumstances. In fact, nobody really understood what was going on. How could Angela possibly explain something like this? After all, it was unheard of. So, your daughter wandered off into a parallel universe, are you kidding me? Angela knew what the reactions would be from most people when hearing something like that. The majority of people would express disbelief or the notion that she was completely crazy or had fallen prey to some conspiracy theory so bizarre that she was the only proponent of it.

She appreciated how patient Bill was with her and yet she wished he, of all people, could at the very least pretend to believe her. There was no way to really explain what had happened. And so Angela had fallen into telling a comfortable lie about her daughter to most people, including her parents. When asked about her, Angela explained truthfully that her daughter Charli had "moved away, a long way away," and she was enjoying her life and probably would not return. Angela was able to genuinely express her sadness she couldn't spend time with Charli, while at the same time hoping she was having a good life. It was when she was pressed on the "where" that she tended to stumble. Sometimes she would say Charli was in a job where she "moved around a lot" and she "wasn't quite sure where she is at the moment." Sometimes she would describe Charli being in a place that was as far away as she could possibly imagine like New Zealand or the Arctic Circle.

Gradually, people became accustomed to the fact Angela was now estranged from her first daughter, but she was consoled by the prospect of her second child. The questions gradually ceased, and friends and co-workers started to talk about other things.

Angela had been let go from her job as an elementary school teacher during the pandemic, and her temporary job as a cashier at Ingles did little to fulfill her or support her. So, when she met Bill and he offered to support her financially, Angela had taken the opportunity to follow one of her passions, which was to work with young children.

She got a child development certification and worked part-time as a substitute teacher at a local elementary school. This type of position was one she enjoyed enormously. She loved the way she could be a part of a young child's life when it was on the cusp of finding out what life was all about for the first time.

Bill had gone to work, and it was one of Angela's half-days, so she was busy cleaning the house and trying to take her mind off her sadness, which was a regular focus of hers. She asked Alexa to play some "country music" and she hummed along to the tunes she knew so well, as she dusted and vacuumed. She wanted to prove that, despite her shifting moods these days, she was a good woman and would eventually be a good wife to Bill and he would be a good husband to her.

Before now, she had not dared to enter Charli's room. Something about it was too close to her emotions and had the potential to trigger those feelings of despondency she was trying to avoid. But today, she decided it was time to tackle her fears and enter the room. It was November and two months since that fateful day when Charli had run into the living room with a wild expression and a pleading voice asking her mother to join her in "another world." It was time to put the past behind her and move on into the next phase of her life. The best way to do that was to clean out her daughter's things rather than keeping them in this enforced shrine nobody was allowed to enter.

She pushed open the door with a strange trepidation as if she thought a ghost would be behind it or some unknown mysterious force that would leap out and attack her. Behind the door, there were no surprises. The room was just as Charli had left it and exactly as Angela remembered it. In fact, Charli had only spent a couple of days back home in her room before she disappeared for four months, and then suddenly appeared again in a state of extreme dishevelment and emotional disarray that was most alarming.

Since Charli still had friends in the area from before starting college, Angela assumed she was visiting them when she'd mysteriously vanished from her mother's home. Angela was therefore shocked to learn from Charli that she had been somewhere much stranger and more mysterious—a whole other "parallel universe."

At first, Angela thought Charli was using drugs again, so wild was her exterior and frantic her mood. Charli swore she was completely sober, and she understood how difficult this must be to grasp but she was telling the truth. Angela was starting to realize she had to believe her, especially now that there had been no word at all from Charli for four months. Nobody else had any clue where she might be. The story of the "other world" seemed a little more possible although still hard to believe.

The first thing Angela noticed when she walked into the room was the plant Charli was growing in a pot by the window. When the plant was small, Charli kept it encased in glass or plastic, something about the "air being toxic" that Angela didn't understand at all. But more recently, the plant had gotten so big it was almost like a small tree and too large to remain inside the room. Angela therefore decided to take it out of the room and move it to her backyard. This move was more difficult than expected, but she managed to get it outside Charli's bedroom and into the hallway but not down the stairs as it was too heavy. She planned to ask Bill to help her with it after he got home from work that evening.

Like her daughter had done a few months earlier, Angela noticed this tree was now growing some fruit from its many branches. The small, orange-colored balls hanging down like Christmas tree ornaments enticed Angela to rub one between her fingers and feel its smooth glossy skin. In her enthusiasm, she managed to pluck the fruit and hold it up to the light momentarily so she could study it further. Then she put it into her pocket.

The next task was to sort through Charli's things and decide what to keep and what to throw away. She didn't have many clothes in her closet, as most of her things were still in Raleigh at the apartment she shared with her roommate. Angela had no idea what to do about that situation, and assumed Charli had made some arrangement before disappearing.

There were a few papers on the desk by Charli's computer, and Angela put them into neat orderly piles and threw out anything resembling trash. When Angela opened up Charli's computer and looked on her social media pages, it was evident the girl hadn't posted anything in the past six months, so obviously this "world" she'd gone to, wherever it was, did not have access to social media. Maybe she'd gone to a monastery?

Angela noticed a small hardbacked book with a purple cover and the word "journal" in large curly letters that Charli liked to use when she was being artistic. Angela felt a little nervous about opening it, fearing rebuke from her daughter even though she was no longer present. Her curiosity got the better of her, and she sat down on Charli's bed and opened up the pages.

Angela learned about Q'ehazi and the true nature of Charli's connection to that place. Her sadness deepened as she realized the extent of the divide between them, the fact this was something she would never share with her daughter, and that it was of great and life-changing value to Charli. The journal went back five years to the first time Charli discovered Q'ehazi. Angela discovered everything that had happened to her daughter there and why it was so significant.

She learned about the *Pukatl* tree and why Charli cherished and protected it so lovingly. She learned about Charli's feelings for Joslyn and her confusion over those feelings for a person who she believed she might never see again.

The only thing Angela didn't learn was what happened to Charli between the time she left for her penultimate trip to Q'ehazi and the afternoon that she had shown up again at home with that panicked expression and the pleas for Angela to accompany her back to the "other world."

As Angela read the journal, a lot of things became clearer. She wished with all her heart she had believed in her daughter more or that her daughter had felt safer to confide in her. Angela felt a sense of responsibility that perhaps she hadn't been a good enough mother because her daughter chose to hide from her something so momentous until it was too late and there was no turning back. She understood now why Charli was so desperate in that moment and why she kept repeating, "The portal is closing. I have to get back there before it closes forever."

Angela wished fervently her daughter valued her time in her own world as much as she did in the world of Q'ehazi, but she could see why Charli made her final decision. Charli had always been so idealistic and so passionate about what she felt was fair and right, and this world had never seemed to live up to Charli's standards in that regard. Angela, on the other hand, was much more accepting and passive about taking things as they were and learning to live life on its terms.

After reading her daughter's journal, Angela had one wish to visit the place that Charli mentioned was the "portal" into the other world—the Redbud Tree by the creek. Angela wondered if there would be something special about this tree that she could recognize or if it would just seem like an ordinary tree to anybody who didn't know its significance.

Angela experienced again the guilt of realizing she maybe hadn't been the best mother to Charli, as she'd been so young and so lost when she'd given birth to her first daughter. She had a belief, though, this time with this baby would be different. Now she had a good job, a good man, and the wisdom she'd gained over the past few years, she could be a much better mother to the child that was growing inside her. She made a promise right then to be the best mother she could be to this new child, whatever and whoever it may be.

Angela wished there was some way she could explain all of this to Charli. She couldn't write her a letter, send her an email or a text, or call her on the phone. Her daughter was gone forever, as completely as if she had died. Yet nobody else could know the severity of the loss she felt because her daughter hadn't died. She had gone to a place where she was unreachable. Angela wanted to tell Charli that her life was good and she was happy. It wasn't Charli's fault, of course, but Angela had never been happy as a young mother to her first daughter. She was so young, and everything was so fraught with danger and uncertainty, confusion, and insecurity.

All she could do now was "speak" to Charli in her own mind and hope that somehow Charli would know what Angela was thinking and feeling. There was always a bond between mother and daughter that could never be broken no matter how tenuous the connection. Angela reassured herself with the thought Charli had told her she was "very happy" in the new world she'd joined, and Angela had to be grateful for that and to know her daughter was safe and well.

Later that day before Bill arrived home, Angela discovered a hard little bump in her pocket and remembered the fruit she inadvertently picked from the strange tree in her daughter's room. She removed it from her pocket and studied it once more, then took it into the kitchen and put it on the chopping board. When she sliced into the fruit with one of her small chopping knives, she was surprised to find that the inside flesh was quite soft and a pinkish color. Unwilling to bite into something when she had no idea what it was, Angela carefully scooped out a little of the flesh with a teaspoon and popped a small bit of it into her mouth. To her surprise, it was actually a very pleasant taste. So she removed all of the flesh from around the inner seeds and discarded the seeds and the skin.

As Angela enjoyed the rest of the fruit, she heard Bill's key turn in the lock of the front door. Almost as if she were relishing some guilty pleasure she didn't want her partner to know about, Angela quickly swallowed the rest of her prize and washed the telltale signs of fruit from her chopping board just in time before Bill entered the kitchen. Then she turned to Bill and welcomed him with a smile only partly due to her happiness about seeing him again at the end of what had been a long and tumultuous day.

Chapter Twenty-One

In the spring of the following year, Charli's daughter was born. She had a mass of curly black hair, creamy brown skin, and dark iridescent blue eyes. The little baby looked up at Charli and Joslyn with an expression that was both innocent and wise and seemed to say, "I'm here now, all is well." Everyone remarked on the unique beauty of the little girl who Charli named Caspera.

In keeping with Q'ehazi tradition, there was both a naming and a song ceremony a few days after the baby's birth. All the villagers gathered at the sacred Honor Stone, and they each came to view the baby and to lay a tender hand on her cheek in celebration of her birth. Two singers from the Village of Musicians were chosen to compose a song especially for Caspera, and they sang it at the ceremony and taught it to everyone in the village so they could sing it together. The little girl listened and her eyes opened wide in awe and amazement at this welcoming ceremony that was just for her.

Although Charli and Joslyn were the biological parents of this baby, the whole village was tasked with raising her in keeping with Q'ehazi tradition. Parents were not regarded as "owners" of their children any more than they were owners of the air they breathed or the life-giving water that fell from the sky each day.

More than anybody else, Caspera was her own creator. After the first few months of breast-feeding, which was a duty unique to Charli, family friends and extended family members from Joslyn's clan were allocated to care for little Caspera. It was considered a superior form of raising a baby, as the child was introduced to many different personalities and ways of being, and that gave it a much more well-rounded perspective on life and behavior.

Aurora and Serano participated as the grandparents, but they were not the only ones who helped raise Caspera. Everybody aided in imbuing the child with a sense of shared values and customs that were so important to the Q'ehazi people. As an only child, she was exposed to other children her own age from the earliest time of her existence, and this helped to socialize her and turn her into a little girl who was very comfortable being with others, as well as being alone when the time was right. Her personality was a joyful one, even as a small baby, and a sense of wonder and a happy awe at the world were within her from the start.

Epilogue

The hummingbird landed on the yellow flower and pecked at the nectar contained in its petals, alternately raising its head as if to swallow the sweet juice and then dipping again for more. It flew in a cloud of effervescent wing flaps, and it hovered in the air as if weightless, suspended aloft only by speed and relentless energy. Caspera watched the little bird, utterly fascinated, her mouth agape in wonder. Then as the tiny creature flew to a more distant flower, she followed, enjoying this chasing game and giggling in delight. Just a few more feet, then the bird moved again to quench its thirst at another bloom and then another and another. Caspera giggled and followed until the bird flew off and was lost to view. Turning around, she realized she had now gotten so far distant from her friends she could no longer see them behind her. But she was enjoying herself too much to be afraid. Her natural curiosity led her to explore this new area that she'd never been in before.

Caspera lived in the Village of Healers Southeast with her parents, and they had traveled to this area to visit with her grandmother, Sovereign Aurora. Since school was over for the day, she'd been playing with some of the older children who were local to that area. They had started playing the Q'ehazi game, which Caspera was a little too young to understand, and because of this she'd become distracted by the bird, and now found herself far from home and from anybody she knew. But with the enduring faith of a six-year-old child who has always been loved and protected by its parents and the whole village, Caspera never considered herself in any danger, and she just assumed when the time was right she'd either find her way back to them or they would find her.

And so she skipped along the ground, enjoying the beautiful warm sunshine as it fell on her coffee-colored skin and the feel of the gentle breeze as it ruffled her mass of curly black hair. Sometimes she was entranced by the colorful wildflowers dotting the path, and sometimes by the trees that were new to her. Caspera knew the names of all the trees by her home, but she had not seen any of these before, and some of them had shapes and sizes she'd never seen. There was one where two trees emerged from the same trunk, as if they were twins born at the exact same time. And here was another with scratchy bark dotted with patches of smooth green moss.

Caspera skipped along, taking in all the sights and sounds, and singing softly to herself. Her song had been written for her to celebrate her birth, and she knew it by heart and enjoyed singing it, especially when she was alone.

Now she heard an unusual sound, and she cocked an ear to try and distinguish it better. It was a rushing, liquid sort of sound, a sort of tinkling that reminded her of when mama ran her a bath in the big tub inside the longhouse. She followed the sound as she had followed the little bird earlier, needing to solve the mystery of what could produce such a sound out here in the wilderness, where she imagined no tubs existed.

In a few minutes, the trees cleared, and she could see what was making the noise. It was water, but water like she'd never seen before because it was cascading over rocks and pebbles and forming a stream like a small river. *Perhaps this is what Daddy calls a creek,* she thought to herself as she stood by the stream admiring the way the water formed itself into little pools and rivulets and left the pebbles beneath it so smooth and shiny with wetness.

As she stood there in a trance-like stillness, a small bird alighted on her shoulder and deftly pecked at her ear, causing her to giggle as she felt the tickle of its beak. This was not an unusual occurrence for Caspera. She had inherited from her father the almost uncanny connection with animals and birds and trees that caused other people in the village to refer to her as "the animal wrangler."

In fact, one day, while out walking in the forest with her mother, they had both come across a long, black snake lying across their path. Although her mother had leapt back in horror and fear, the little girl had remained calm and open, simply telling "Mr. Snake" to "go about your business" and watching as the creature slithered peacefully away under the bushes.

When Caspera moved again and started to walk by the shores of the creek, the bird remained stubbornly on her shoulder as if it had found a temporary home. In a few steps, Caspera came across a tree unlike anything she'd ever seen before and that was remarkably different from the others.

This tree was tall and dark with no branches. On its trunk had been carved intricate decorations that were quite beautiful pictures of stars and moons and birds and animals. Caspera was at an age where she still believed in magic, and she wondered if this was a magic tree. It didn't occur to her perhaps these symbols had been deliberately carved on the tree by another human being since she had never heard of such a thing. The pictures, in her child's imagination, must have been created by the tree itself.

Caspera was so fascinated by this tree she rubbed its intricate carvings with her fingers, trying to see if they would feel rough or smooth to the touch. The little bird was still on her shoulder, although by now it had stopped pecking at her ear and seemed to be just watching, wondering what she'd do next.

All of a sudden, the strangest sensation came over her, unlike anything she'd ever felt before. It was a little similar to the sensation she felt when Auntie Abbe whirled her round playfully and she screamed in delight as she saw the world turning around her or when she woke up in the morning and her eyes were a little foggy and her thoughts "soggy" as she called it, from sleep. It was not an unpleasant sensation, but it was disorientating. In front of her there seemed to be a curtain like the curtain of a stage before the performance begins. So Caspera had the idea that if she stepped through this curtain, she could see the show, and so she did step through, the little bird on her shoulder, as if it too were wanting to see what would happen next.

What did happen next was that Caspera stepped through the filmy curtain and into the other world. She didn't at this time know this was the other world her own mother had ventured from or that her own maternal grandmother still inhabited. But she did realize she was no longer in her own world of Q'ehazi, and being as imaginative like most children, she assumed that some magic had transported her here.

The air felt denser, thicker, and as she breathed in, she was aware it took a little more effort to breathe here. The colors around her were a little darker than those at home. When she looked up at the sky, it was still blue but a different kind of blue, more of a blue-gray as if was streaked with clouds. She could hear dogs barking in the distance, and this was a surprising sound, one she was not unfamiliar with, but back home dogs only barked when they were in pain or needed something and then only for a short while, whereas here their barking was constant. The trees were still there, and the creek in the same position, but off in the distance she could make out the contours of buildings that decorated the landscape, and this was very different from home. She still heard bird songs, but they were less clear and vibrant than she was used to.

Caspera was suddenly aware that her little bird friend had fallen off her shoulder and was now lying on the ground. She bent down to see what the matter was, and she was horrified to see that the little bird was opening and closing its beak as if gasping for breath, its tiny wings fluttering in distress, and its eyes wide open, as if struggling to keep a hold on life.

Caspera would have stayed and investigated further, but she had a powerful intuition the bird was suffering precisely because she had inadvertently brought it into this place where it couldn't survive. The only way to save it would be to return to Q'ehazi immediately and so this is what she did.

She picked up the tiny creature carefully in her hands and stepped back through the curtain where everything was the same and yet completely different. She cradled the little bird and said soothing words to it to try and coax it back to life. But it was too late. The bird was already dead.

Tears stung the corners of her eyes as she did the ritual over the bird that she had been taught by her father and dug a small grave for it in the ground where she placed it ceremoniously.

Now she glanced back at the tree, the uncommon black tree with its carvings, and the same fascination with this other world permeated her, but she knew she would need to come back later, much later, when she was no longer a child and could navigate her way through this world successfully and without harming any other creatures along the way.

Caspera's normal mood of lightness and joy returned as she retraced her steps back to the place she had come from earlier that day. And when she saw the fringes of her grandmother's village and the inhabitants going about their business, her heart lifted in anticipation of whatever life ahead would hold for her and her family.

In her child's brain she had formed a plan, a new plan. She would not tell anyone about the adventure she'd had today. But she would find a way to return to this spot one day when she was older and she knew more, much more about life. She would travel through the curtain again to see what was beyond. If there truly was another world there, a world beyond this one that she knew, she was going to find it, and maybe she'd find her other grandmother there, too.

As she walked, she became aware of two large butterflies with bright orange wings who were circling and chasing each other across the tops of the trees. Caspera stopped momentarily, her mouth agape in wonder, as she followed the antics of the little creatures swooping and hovering in the air in front of her. Then suddenly, both butterflies flew toward her and landed on her chest, one on either side of her heart and remained there as if stuck to her. They were so big and she was so small, they formed a sort of adornment to her little girl dress, which was her favorite shade of kingfisher blue, so that the vivid color of the butterflies stood out as if they were decorative fixtures.

Caspera's arrival at the village and her return among her friends who were still engaged in playing the Q'ehazi Game drew some delighted stares and comments from the villagers as they recognized the little girl's new "adornments" were actually living creatures who had chosen to be there, albeit momentarily. After a few people prodded the butterflies with their fingers to check if they were real, the little creatures eventually flew off among the trees. Caspera continued to smile in her uniquely serene way, when prompted by questions such as "How did those things get there?"

For many years after that, Caspera was known affectionately in the village as Butterfly Girl, and she recognized that day as being one of the most significant of her young life. Not only because of the butterfly visitation, but because of her discovery of the other world that she knew in her heart she would return to again once she was ready. She told no one of her discovery, but she knew there was some reason why she had been chosen to experience the other world, and she was meant to experience something there one day, though she knew not what.

Appendices

These appendices were created by Angela Speranza James in 2025, following her discovery of the book brought back from Q'ehazi by her daughter.

APPENDIX ONE—
THE QEHAZI GAME: The Game Where Everybody Wins

WHAT THE GAME TEACHES THE PLAYERS

- To the Q'ehazi people, the notion of competition means using the energy of each other's performance to enhance one's own; it does not imply that we should crush our opponents or try to win at any cost.
- When we choose to gain at the expense of another person, we are not operating at optimum efficiency. The Q'ehazi believe that survival of the individual at the expense of the whole threatens the survival of the whole—which incidentally includes the individual.
- Symbiosis, which is the assembly of individuals based on mutually beneficial relationships, is a major driving force behind evolution.
- Life did not take over the globe by combat but by networking.

- The Old Way: I win; you lose. You win; I lose. The New Way: Transcendence happens when the problem is solved by avoiding it entirely. Compromise, and each person wins by agreeing to lose a little. Transcendence produces a resolution above and beyond the problem.
- There is a Value to Interdependence, and everybody has an important role to play. Some analogies and metaphors are as follows: a machine where all parts need to work in order for the machine to operate or a play where all players are necessary, from the bit parts to the leading roles. If a boat is crossing the ocean and encounters a storm, everybody needs to pull together in order for everyone to make it.
- Money is not the most valuable commodity to acquire. It is the Gold Stars or Karma cards that are the most valuable commodity to acquire because they demonstrate what you have truly achieved in the life of the Game. You only acquire these things by giving away things or doing good deeds to help others.

APPENDIX TWO—
THE Q'EHAZI STORY by Professor Ben Avendo

Q'EHAZI HISTORY

The long history of an oral tradition that preserves the stories of the Q'ehazi people means that we are able to trace back their ancestry to almost the dawn of civilization. What we know with relative certainty is that a few people from one tribe migrated from the far south to the islands close to the equator around the time of Jesus' birth. These were the Arawaks, who settled and lived in peaceful harmony for many centuries, mostly deriving their living from fishing and harvesting small crops of the abundant tropical fruits such as coconuts, mangoes, plantain, breadfruit, etc.

In the early 1500s, the warlike Caribs invaded these islands, and many of the peaceful Arawaks were slaughtered; a small band of them managed to escape and headed north, where they settled on the shores of the northerly continent we now know as Pacifica, which stretched from the Atlantic coast on the east to the Pacific coast on the west and was a vast and untapped land at that time inhabited by many diverse native tribes.

These Arawaks settled and started to form a new life for themselves here in these more northerly climes. As they were on the coast, they managed to continue using their skills at fishing and harvesting crops, although the food they planted now changed to vegetables such as corn, sweet potatoes, and yams. The most important thing the Arawaks brought with them was the seed of their culture, which was one of peace and harmony and a respect for all living things. Gradually, as they merged with the peoples of the area they now inhabited, they began to adopt some new customs as well as maintaining some of their own.

With this, they formed a new people, and they called themselves the Q'ehazi, which is an old Arawak term meaning "peace" or "harmony". They lived in what they called a Maca Bana, which is their word for "tree dwelling". The Q'ehazi also began using a local herb called the Pukatl, which came from a locally grown tree. This herb enabled them not only to survive disease and maintain optimum levels of emotional stability, but it also helped them to calm any others who came within their reach or who attempted to take them over or corrupt their way of life. It was the use of this herb on a regular basis, coupled with a societal system that valued community over individualism, that taught a respect for all nature and managed and controlled both procreation and child-rearing that formed the basis for the successful and gradual growth of the Q'ehazi peoples into what it is today—a flourishing and thriving society and economy where all members are able to live a harmonious and happy life.

One of the main challenges the Q'ehazi faced early on was the visit to their shores of a small band of English would-be colonists, who arrived on a ship led by Sir Walter Raleigh in 1563. For some months, the future of the Q'ehazi tribe—at that time relatively new to the area and lacking in substance or population—hung in the balance, as the incoming settlers could have provided either a threat or a benefit to them. But ultimately, the two groups merged peacefully and harmoniously and recognized that they both would profit from living together in harmony rather than with one group attempting to control the other.

The people intermarried and became as one. After several generations, they were indistinguishable. The Europeans brought with them skills related to metal production, writing, and mathematics, and systems of government. For their part, the natives possessed skills related to their lifestyle such as fishing and harvesting crops and the mining of gems, as well as information about their local plants that were good for growing, harvesting, and eating. The natives also knew a lot about medicinal herbs that were good for healing all sorts of ailments, the local animals, the flora and fauna, and their type of religion, which was really a form of nature deity. Both groups blended together in perfect harmony. They also intermarried and formed the modern-day ancestors of the Q'ehazi people.

This new and more developed white/red tribe of people successfully infiltrated and influenced all of the other tribes on the continent, and eventually "took over" the entire continent with their ideas and not by force. They never did anything by force, but they did everything by persuasion. Their ideas were so powerful and persuasive that others wished to follow them. Life was good for the Q'ehazi, and others wished to have such a peaceful, harmonious, and productive life. When warring tribes tried to kill and rape them, the Q'ehazi people turned them around with love and peaceful means. "Love always wins over hate and fear" is one of their favorite mottoes.

The Q'ehazi flourished and grew, and eventually, after many generations—always using the gentle art of persuasion (with the help of the Pukatl herb) rather than force—permeating the whole continent, which they now called Pacifica.

In the 1700s, other travelers heard about the success of the Q'ehazi society and started coming to Pacifica's shores. They were not only travelers from Europe and Asia but also from Africa. The Q'ehazi people always welcomed everyone, no matter what their ethnicity or color, so long as they were committed to maintaining the peaceful and harmonious society they had entered. These travelers were given absolute 100% citizenship in exchange for helping build infrastructure and contributing in whatever way they could to the new society. They also had total rights to intermarry with the Q'ehazi people and create an even stronger blend of racial characteristics. So now that the black African people were intermarried with them, the Q'ehazi people had all of those characteristics, too, such as a great ability to run and play sports and a sense of rhythm and dance. The Q'ehazi people also welcomed and incorporated the Asian cultures, who they admired for their intelligence and dedication to community. Another group, the Jewish cultures, were admired for their productivity and work ethic.

All of the cultures were woven together and the best parts of them were taken into the Q'ehazi society, so that it became like a strong and colorfully blended cloth. The Q'ehazi had a way of representing this visually that was passed down through the generations. It was a sacred ceremonial shawl woven of many colors that was worn by many women in the Q'ehazi society as a symbol of their recognition of the rich tapestry they had inherited.

The Q'ehazi culture is one that believes it is stronger when it adapts. The original mission is never forgotten, which incorporates ideas such as "all human beings are created equal" that are contained in the original Q'ehazi manifesto written in the 1600s and adhered to ever since. (This original document is kept in a safe place and can be viewed by modern-day descendants and visitors.)

Now, in the 21st century, this is the history on which the Q'ehazi rest.

Q'EHAZI BELIEFS

It is the Q'ehazi belief that if you are not spiritually connected to the Earth and understand the spiritual reality of how to live on Earth, it is likely that you will not survive. Everything is spiritual, everything has a spirit, everything was brought here by the creator, the one creator. Some people call this God, while other people speak of Buddha, Allah, and other names. The Q'ehazi call this the Great Spirit. Humans are here on Earth only a few winters then they go to the spirit world.

There is a need for understanding but not for vengeance, and a need for reparation but not for retaliation. Society, not a transcendent being, gives human beings their humanity, and humanity comes from conforming to or being part of society. Humanity is a quality we owe to each other. We create each other and need to sustain this otherness creation. If we belong to each other, we participate in our creations.

The Q'ehazi people believe in hugging strangers, because once you've had that kind of physical touch with somebody, it's much harder to think of them as "the enemy". There is sincere warmth with which people treat both strangers and members of the community. This overt display of warmth is not merely aesthetic but enables the formation of spontaneous communities.

Our philosophy encourages community equality and promoting the distribution of abundance. We believe that everyone has different skills and strengths; people are not isolated, and through mutual support, they can help each other to complete themselves.

Our notion of redemption relates to how people deal with errant, deviant, and dissident members of the community. The belief is that men and women are born formless like a lump of clay. It is up to the community, as a whole, to use the fire of experience and the wheel of social control to make a pot that may contribute to society.

The Q'ehazi Manifesto talks about the spiritual and ethical beliefs of the people: That every person is created equal, no matter what their gender or skin color; that the highest aim of every person is to do good and to attain a State of Grace; that the health of the community as a whole is as important as the health of the individual (because it creates the health of the individual, and the two are interdependent); that all living beings are to be valued; that it is important to live in harmony with the rest of nature.

All Q'ehazi people are brought up from an early age to eat and/or drink the medicinal herb that gives them their gentle, pacifist nature. When disputes happen, they are always resolved without violence. There is no such thing as money and no one person has power over another person. There is no hierarchy, and the people who lead do it to serve. Fairness is the most important aspect.

Mother Earth must be respected and honored as the living being that she is, and all beings in Nature honored and left alone in their natural habitat. Their energy must be allowed to resonate freely throughout the Universe as it should for healing to come to the world.

We Are All One, just like cells in a body make up the whole body, and when some cells are sick that means the whole body is sick. In exactly the same way, the whole of humanity, the whole of the world cannot be healthy unless every single being within it is healthy.

Q'ehazi people want to take care of their own body, mind, and spirit because they have healthy self-esteem. Because people have meaningful and pleasant lives, they never need to abuse things like drugs, alcohol, and prescription medications.

The Q'ehazi realize that we are all here together in order to live a meaningful existence. Every person has value, it is up to them to recognize and express what that value may be. Everybody is different but everybody has value. An artist has value, a doctor has value, a crazy person has value, a sick person has value. People who fix people are the most valuable of all—therapists, healers, and doctors.

The Q'ehazi people know that every single person is a valuable treasure that is to be taken care of and nurtured, body, mind, and soul. Only then can the whole world be healthy and whole, when every person is treasured. If we have just one sick and suffering person in the world, then we are all sick.

For our Q'ehazi people, status is acquired not by money—which is worthless in our eyes—but by giving things away. Thus, we have a ceremony in which the goal is to give away as much as possible. That is the way prestige is achieved.

The Q'ehazi people are born with an obligation to give back and to pay it forward. It is a way of maintaining balance, repaying favors, and doing good for others. We know that balance is essential for human survival, and they live this every day and in every facet of their society.

The future of our Earth—the environment—is our responsibility. How we transport ourselves and how we heat and light our homes are major force factors in protecting our Earth. We know that a part of our domain is the production of the food we eat. We can optimize our health by eating food free of poisons that we grow ourselves.

The three basics of the Q'ehazi calling are:

(1) The giving of gifts—The gifts of the people in our neighborhood are boundless.
(2) The power of association—In association we join our gifts together and they become amplified, magnified, productive, and celebrated.
(3) Hospitality—We welcome strangers because we value their gifts and need to share our own. Our doors are open.

APPENDIX THREE—
YOUR TURN

NOW IT'S YOUR TURN TO CONTRIBUTE TO THE Q'EHAZI' ONGOING STORY.

THIS BOOK IS THE SECOND OF A TRILOGY THAT WILL BE COMPLETED IN THE COMING MONTHS AND YEARS.

CAN YOU IMAGINE A BETTER WORLD? IF WE CAN VISUALIZE IT TOGETHER, PERHAPS WE CAN COLLECTIVELY MANIFEST IT.

YOU CAN SET UP Q'EHAZI GROUPS, WHERE YOU DISCUSS HOW A MORE IDEAL WORLD WOULD LOOK, AND WHAT IT WOULD TAKE TO GET THERE.

YOU CAN COME UP WITH YOUR OWN IDEAS ON HOW TO CREATE A PERFECT WORLD, AND WE CAN CONTINUE TO MODIFY AND ADD TO THE VISION IN FUTURE Q'EHAZI BOOKS.

YOU CAN HAVE FUN USING YOUR OWN CREATIVITY AND WISDOM TO IMAGINE HOW THE WORLD COULD BE BETTER.

STAY CONNECTED

www.yourworldbeyond.com -
Keep up with events related to all books in the trilogy.

info@yourworldbeyond.com -
Send an email to join the newsletter.

Join the newsletter to keep informed
about the third book in the trilogy
and book events near you.

FACEBOOK -
https://www.facebook.com/profile.php?id=100084508364041

ALL BOOKS BY THIS AUTHOR -
http://www.madisoncbrightwell.com

POST A REVIEW ON Amazon / Goodreads / Barnes and Noble

You can purchase Book One in the trilogy, as a Kindle eBook, paperback, or hardback edition, or as an Audible book, and read many reviews, by going to this Amazon link:

https://www.amazon.com/World-Beyond-Redbud-Tree-ebook/dp/B0BW7SKN38

www.ingramcontent.com/pod-product-compliance
Lightning Source LLC
LaVergne TN
LVHW041712070526
838199LV00045B/1311